I0612149

THE EAGLE'S HAMMER

THE EAGLE'S HAMMER

CHRISTOPHER KÜGLER

KLOCKWORK PUBLISHING
Bellefonte, Pennsylvania

Copyright © 2021 by Christopher Kugler

This is a work of fiction. All names, places, and characters — including those based on real people, living or dead — as well as characterizations and opinions are products of the author's imagination or are used fictitiously. Locales and public names are sometimes used for atmospheric purposes. Any resemblance to actual people, businesses, companies, events, institutions, or locales is completely fictitious or coincidental.

All rights reserved. No part of this publication may be reproduced, distributed or transmitted in any form or by any means, including photocopying, recording, or other electronic or mechanical methods, without the prior written permission of the publisher, except in the case of brief quotations embodied in critical reviews and certain other noncommercial uses permitted by copyright law.

Klockwork Publishing
www.klockworkpublishing.com

ISBN: 978-1-7349869-6-9
Ebook ISBN: 978-1-7349869-7-6

To Chuba: the best costar I ever had.

PROLOGUE

America, 2073
Lights • Camera • Violence

The studio lights fade up and bathe the two attractive news anchors in as bright and flattering a light as money can buy. The anchorman, his hair slicked back and perfect, he looks at their camera as if it insulted them. "America," he says, all business. "Our country is under attack."

The anchorwoman, her backlight casting an angelic crown upon her blonde perm, turns to another camera, her single. "Crime is out of control," she says, urgent.

"Sins are being committed," the man says, now glaring at his own camera.

"And our children are in danger," the woman says, pleading.

Together, they turn to the original camera, the two-shot. "But rest easy, patriots," the man says, suddenly reassuring.

"Because *The Eagle's Hammer*," the woman says, all smiles.

"Is about to drop," they say together, triumphant.

Cue the slick-as-hell opening montage, complete with such mesmerizing effects and up-tempo music that you can't help but stare at your screen transfixed. The barrage of images and sounds introduces you to *The Eagle's Hammer*, a celebrated but unflinchingly violent paramilitary death squad consisting of six members who have pledged absolute loyalty to the laws of the land.

You, the viewer at home, you watch this program every night as the team hunts down and murders alleged criminals, live for all to see. Not because you want to watch, but because you have to. It's the law. This show, *The Eagle's Hammer*, it's the longest-running series in history. And no matter where you are or what you're doing, you hold your phone to your face, let the recognition software confirm your identity, and watch that night's public execution... all the while praying you're not their next target.

Back in the studio, a rogue's gallery of expert commentators, network pundits, and celebrity guests spit out mindless commentary and delusional, brainwashed drivel as infographics explain the target's ludicrous crimes. Unauthorized drug use, fake news propagation, unlicensed adultery: the list goes on and on, each *'crime'* more absurd than the last.

"Justice," one such pundit says, starry-eyed. "This is justice, and I love it."

Now, you might be saying to yourself: this sounds like a twenty-first-century public flogging. And you'd be right. That's exactly what this is. And, if you're feeling left out of the fun, a chyron graphic scrolling across the screen beacons you to go ahead and report a crime yourself — anonymously, of course. Your neighbor, your brother, your husband... sure, turn 'em in. And the best part is you get first dibs on their personal property, minus what they owe their creditors, of course. But as for their savings accounts and retirement portfolios: that goes straight to Uncle Sam. *To the benefit of the greater good.*

But how, you ask?

What about the Bill of Rights?

What about the Constitution?

Well, after a domestic terrorist attack left Washington D.C. a radioactive ash heap, not many gave pause for *our rights*, not when those responsible were still out there, threatening to do it again. Operating outside the periphery of the nation's law enforcement and intelligence apparatus,

The Eagle's Hammer — both the team and entertainment program — was the brainchild of the Trucast Corporation, the country's largest internet provider and content producer.

The pitch was simple: find and punish those responsible for destroying the nation's capital, and broadcast it all in hopes of mending the public's broken psyche. The show, the network promised, would be cathartic. For the acting president at the time, the decision was a no-brainer. The executive order was hastily signed, and *The Eagle's Hammer* took flight.

Now, decades later, you're sitting in your living room, your husband by your side, watching as the team's super-sonic scramjet lands within their target's city limits — it looks to be Baltimore, and you breathe a sigh of relief: they're not after you, not tonight. A cargo ramp extends, and each team member charges out in their own heavily armored hammermobile...

Yes, they're called hammermobiles. And the public obsession with them is fanatical.

Racing off toward their target, a dozen autonomous drones chase after them, ultra-def cameras mounted on top. Following the team's every move, these hover-cams are programmed to frame up the best shot and uplink the footage back to the network's production facilities where, like any major sporting event, the video is paired with

commentators in the studio. From there, the broadcast
is blasted out to each and every streaming device in the
United States… or what's left of it, at least.

As for the team itself, each *hammer*, as they're popularly
called, was raised and trained since childhood for this sole
purpose. Talented, loyal, and drop-dead gorgeous, each
hammer is perfection incarnate. Male, female, non-binary;
they're a testament to the modern age. But of these six
specimens, one stands out from the rest: Taylor Evans.

As the official face of *The Eagle's Hammer*, Evans is
a celebrity phenomenon who, depending on whom you
ask — and what surveillance devices might be present — is
either a national hero… or a coldblooded monster.

He gets the close-up, again and again.

And he gets the kill, night after night.

Way back when you first started watching this show,
you were just a kid. And at first, it felt right. It felt necessary. In the beginning, *The Eagle's Hammer* did precisely
what they were supposed to: they hunted down and killed
the terrorists responsible, preventing another catastrophe.
After that, they hunted down and killed the country's most
dangerous, most vile criminals. And that seemed okay, too,
especially when you heard how scary and menacing those
people were. But then they started killing drug dealers. And
then it was drug users. The next thing you knew, they were

executing illegal migrants. Then political dissidents. Then online critics. And before you knew it, they were killing your next-door neighbors right before your eyes.

On your screen, the lead hammermobile skids to a stop in front of a rundown rowhouse of Harlem Park. It's always the low-income neighborhoods, the working class. The machine eats the poor. But we're all poor, the wealthy elites having gobbled up all the wealth, leaving nothing for anybody else. The middle class? There is no middle class, just the haves and have-nots. But we're all stuck in this nightmare together, forever and ever.

As Evans steps out of his car, a hover-cam circles him low and dramatic, creating what the industry likes to call *the hero shot*. Inside, the target — having recognized their city, then their neighborhood, and now their front door — is undoubtedly shitting themself.

With the other hammers joining him, Evans draws his weapon, bringing it near his face as the camera pushes in for a close-up. As the music reaches a crescendo, Evans narrows his eyes and says his iconic catchphrase: "Let's bust 'em."

Sitting between your feet on your living room floor is your own kid, probably the same age you were when you first started watching. Only your kid loves it; he savors it. It's like a religion. With his official Taylor Evans action figure clutched tightly in his little hand, he watches every moment, night after night, unflinching. And as Evans says his line, and as the team smashes through their target's front door, your kid cheers. "Yeah!"

You and your husband, you exchange an uneasy glance as, on-screen, the team sweeps into the house. With military precision, they scan each room they come to. The kitchen: empty. The dining room: empty. In the living room, they find a wall-mounted television streaming the broadcast itself, and the hammers briefly catch a glimpse of themselves watching themselves watching themselves... until the network cuts away to another camera, severing the visual feedback.

Using hand signals, Evans directs the team toward the stairs, and your kid jumps to his feet, excited. *They're always upstairs.* Charging up the flight, the team kicks down each and every bedroom door, finding children hiding in closets, screaming and crying. Your own kid, he watches it all, giddy. *Their terror is his entertainment.* But Evans and the team press on.

Finally, it all comes down to the last door: the bathroom. *It's always the bathroom.* The door is shut, and the lights are off. But you know they're in there. The hammers know they're in there. Hell, the whole goddamn country knows they're in there, freaking out.

Another team member kicks the door open, clearing the way for Evans to enter. Inside, their target cowers in the tub, covering herself with the shower curtain, wide-eyed and desperate. "Please," she says in short, sharp gasps. "Please. No."

But Evans, he says nothing. Instead, he stares at her as he waits for the buzzing hover-cam to position itself just off to the side. And as he levels his handgun at the target, tears streaming down her cheeks, so too does your kid raise his own make-believe gun to his own imaginary target. And just as Evans pulls his trigger, exploding the target's brain onto the white tiles behind her, your kid pulls his trigger…

BAM.

The broadcast cuts back to the studio. And the anchors stare at the camera, euphoric. Another night, another murder. Another job well done.

"God bless *The Eagle's Hammer*," the anchorman says. "And God bless America."

Be sure to like, share, and subscribe, folks.

Or else.

CHAPTER 1

The doors open, and the horde of fans goes wild. They're cheering for me, Taylor Evans. *The* Taylor Evans. Standing with my shoulders square and teeth clenched, I know I look good in the spotlight. Real good.

Me, I'm handsome, healthy, and stoic…

Just like they want.

Just like you want.

You, you're at home watching because your kid loves this shit. Or that's how you play it off, at least. Secretly, you admire everything about me. My chiseled features. My cropped hair. My celebrity lifestyle. Yeah, your kid probably loves me like all kids love their heroes.

But you, you just want me.

To my side are the other five members of *The Eagle's Hammer*, waving to the crowd, flashing smiles, and blowing kisses. But let's not kid ourselves. These people, this fanatical mob with such pathetic lives that they have nothing better to do than wait hours, crowded together, pissing themselves lest they lose their standing spot: they are here for me.

Once the team and I were up in the air, the flight back to the Eagle's Nest was a quick thirty minutes. The autonomous scramjet is capable of supersonic flight, but there's no reason to shatter any windows on the way back, not after the kill.

Back in the old days — before the terrorist attack, before I was even born — the Eagle's Nest was known as McGuire Air Force Base. Now, it's used exclusively as our locker room and launchpad. From there, we can hop to pretty much anywhere we want, landing within minutes after take-off…

It's pretty badass.

A high-speed rail system beneath the ground connects the Eagle's Nest directly to the Trucast Corporation's headquarters, located here in Center City, Philadelphia. The ride is a brisk fifteen minutes. By the time we change out of our body armor and show fatigues, and by the time my teammates finish chugging their champagne, it's roughly been an hour since I put that bullet through our target's head...

Back in Baltimore, her body is still warm.

Here in front of me, camera-units hover at the ready, their lenses black, soul-sucking voids in which I can see my reflection. The network's coverage of *The Eagle's Hammer* never actually ends; the viewers just change how they consume it.

Terror turns to relief. Relief turns to anticipation. Anticipation turns to terror. It is an endless loop from which there's no escape. There's no turning off this content or unfollowing this madness. It is all-consuming and addictive by design. It's the full breadth of human emotion presented in twenty-four-hour cycles.

I take a step forward, and the crowd surges toward me. Their excitement, their anticipation, it means nothing to me. They mean nothing to me. The spotlights mounted from the autonomous hover-units are blinding, but I've trained myself not to squint. Never show weakness; that's the Hammer's way.

These people, they feed off anything that makes me seem more human. If I blink or flinch, they think better of themselves. And we don't want that; we never want that. Pure adulation is a fantastic means of control. Without it, the scales could tip in their favor. Then people would have to die, a lot of them. So, the higher I am on the public's pedestal, the safer the people are. Whether they realize it or not.

Behind me, Trucast Tower climbs fifteen hundred feet into the night sky. From afar, the massive skyscraper is a beacon of light, symbolic of 'The Shining City Upon the Hill' mentality that built it. But up close, its pompous mirror-finish reflects its gloomy surroundings right back at the beholder — and maybe that was the intent.

The CEO's office is eighty-four stories up. *The Eight-Four*, we call it. And if you were up there, in that ultra-modern, glass-encased atrium of an office, and you were to look down, you would see six limos with raised platforms to each — something akin to fashion-show runways.

And if you were up there — like our CEO, Hanna Hernandez, always is, looking down, champagne flute in hand — you would see the throngs of fans hovering around each limo.

But if you were up there, on the Eight-Four — looking down with a critical eye, between sips of Dom Pérignon, sizing up the zeitgeist of the moment — you would know that more fans are lined up along one platform in particular, surrounding one limo specifically...

That limo is my limo.

As we walk out along our sponsor-covered platforms, the crowd becomes ravenous and mad. Keeping them at bay are a few dozen nats — the National Guard. Hidden behind their helmets, these troops are faceless and nameless sentries.

Before they became a permanent fixture of life here in the United States, you didn't always know who might show up armed for another mass shooting. Now you always know... it's the nats themselves. In hopes of staving off any and all urban riots, anything goes — the term hyper-militarized just doesn't do them justice.

For the most part, the nats stay out of our way. The network has more to do with controlling the population en masse than the heavy weaponry they carry around. But the nats — wearing their bright blue fatigues with thin red stripes at their shoulders — they don't like me and the other hammers, but not because of any moral conviction. They're just jealous — here we are, bashing in the same skulls as they are, but we're celebrated for it. They, on the other hand, they do the same dirty deeds, and the public despises them.

As for the public, they know it's fucked up — *The Eagle's Hammer*, the National Guard. They know this is a dystopia. But they're too damn scared to speak up...

Would you?

The other hammers, they stop to sign autographs. They reach out to touch the outstretched hands of their fans. They kiss babies and grope whomever they please. Me, I just keep walking.

The screaming and cheers, it's almost deafening, but I keep my eyes on my limo. One foot in front of the other. Like a machine. The crowd chants my name. They beg for my attention. They offer me their bodies. But I dare not look.

Because the last thing I want to see... *is them.*

In all, there must be a couple of thousand fans here to see me off. They're here every night to see Taylor Evans — their hero, their knight in shining armor — off to his beautiful wife.

What do these fans get from this experience? Is it the spectacle? The fanfare?

Perhaps *The Eagle's Hammer* gives them the distraction they need to ignore their dire realities. Maybe this gives them a class of people — our nightly targets — that they can focus their fear and frustrations upon, of which they can feel superior to.

Or perhaps it is even more straightforward than that. Maybe by being so close to me, by standing so close to this flame, they feel less likely to get burned. Perhaps they have convinced themselves that this fandom, this devotion, is their best chance of survival. Perhaps by being here, it somehow lessens the likelihood that I will come for them tomorrow. Perhaps.

Hundreds of camera phones track me as I approach my limo, the crowd hungry for likes and shares on social media. Like most things these days, the limo is fully autonomous, and the door swings open. A nat stands idly by, his finger on his trigger as he watches me with disdain.

Me, I hesitate a moment to see myself in the reflection of his visor. I see the world distorted in the curve of the glass, sweeping away from me into abstract chaos. But at the center of it all is me, the anchor point. I am the linchpin keeping the world from descending into madness.

I slide into the vehicle, the door closes, and the silence is comforting. Alone, finally.

As the limo pulls away, the people — still desperate to touch me, or see me, or be me — push toward my window. As they pound on the glass, I can't help but look into their dim faces. They stare back at me, their breath fogging the surface. But they can't see me, not through the heavy tint. These people, they have no idea that I'm staring back at them — that they actually have my attention. Their gaze is unfocused and distant, yet unblinking. The spark of life is nonexistent.

And I can't help but note how similar they look to a corpse, just moments after death...

But now, I've made my mistake: I looked at them. With a snap of a finger, the people out there banging on my limo, they're no longer my devoted and loyal super fans. They're now my victims. Dead and brutalized. Hundreds of them. Their faces smashed in. Their brains blown out. It's gruesome and horrific. And I can't look away.

These people, the dead, they haunt me. Inextricably linked, till death — my death — do us part. These people, they stare at me in the face; our eyes locked together.

Me, I'm sitting on the plush leather, my fists clenched, unable to move. It's now my breath, hot and panicked, that's fogging the glass.

The dead, they smile back at me.

Their bloody fingers smear the glass.

And I want to scream.

But I can't scream...

Because I'm Taylor Evans.

CHAPTER 2

The woman is spread out on the leather couch, motionless. Her hair and makeup are a mess. And her short designer skirt barely covers her ass. A plethora of drugs covers the coffee table. Half snorted lines of cocaine, an assortment of methaqualone tablets, a pair of empty tumblers: this was clearly a party of two.

Possession. Adultery. Either of these would be reason enough to kill this woman. *To drop the hammer*, as the saying goes. But this woman isn't just another target; this woman is my wife.

The wall-mounted television is still on, still streaming. And the network hacks — b-list studio anchors stuck with the late shift — are babbling on about how great tonight's program was. How divine and inspiring and uplifting and blah blah blah.

On-screen, the pivotal moment of tonight's broadcast is replayed over and over. The kill shot. The slug between the eyes. The target's brains… one second nested securely in her skull, the next splattered on the bathroom tile.

This woman, the one passed out in front of me, her name is Candis Evans. She's about a foot shorter than me, over a hundred pounds lighter, and her eyes typically sparkle brighter than that diamond ring twisted on her finger. But not tonight; tonight, those eyes are rolled back in her head.

Candis is the network's highest-rated astrologer, hosting her own show every afternoon in which she reads you, the viewer, your daily horoscope. Other program highlights include interviewing/gossiping with her network 'friends' about what life is like being married to me, her beloved husband. They discuss what brand of sunglasses I prefer, what low-calorie diet I'm on, etc. Depending on the current crop of sponsors, the topics change regularly. But the audience eats it up regardless.

This woman, she is everything we are told is beautiful. And yet, despite all that, Candis repulses me. Studying her now, I'm struck by how similar she looks to my victims:

used and abused, dead and abandoned, waiting for the network's cleaners to come and carry away.

Or maybe it's the lack of a tablet in her hand, her face typically buried in its screen as she pours over her social media profiles, obsessively checking her notifications as the likes and shares pour in. Instead, at the moment, there's a peace about her, a serenity. Maybe this *is* her best self.

As for my wife and the scene here in front of me, none of this is unusual. In fact, I can still smell his cologne wafting about our swanky, network-provided, high-rise apartment. We loved each other back in the day. Or at least I think we did. Seven years we've been married, and the news reports of our budding relationship and eventual engagement were certainly convincing. Looking back, I can remember the sweet-nothings we'd whisper to each other, late at night, naked in each other's arms...

Unless that was all just dialogue fed to us off-screen. I don't think we were paying much attention back then, to each other or anything.

Sleeping like this, though, Candis looks like a relatively pleasant human being. Feeling some forgotten affection I have for the woman, I decide to take her to the bedroom. To tuck her in like a good, loving husband.

Sliding my hands beneath her, I feel her warm skin against mine as I pick her up. Cradled in my arms, she again reminds me of tonight's target, curled up and dead in her bathtub...

Tonight's target. I don't even know her name. I can't even remember her crime. How can I do it? Night after night? You have to understand, this isn't something I want to do. It just happens. Like a reflex. Shine a light in your face, your eyes constrict. It's automatic. You put a weapon in my hand and...

You see, when we're out there, when I'm working, I'm so focused on the production: on the lights, the cameras, the pacing. I'm so determined to hit my mark and nail my dialogue that I'm swept away by it, like a leaf in a stream. All that energy, all that adrenaline, there's no getting off that train...

I don't want to kick down that front door... yet I have.

I don't want to place my gun between her eyes... but I do.

At that moment, in that flicker of time in which that human being's life hangs in the balance, all I hear is the show's director in my ear, barking orders. I see my target; I see her mouth moving, pleading. I see the desperation in her face, and I understand it. But that's all part of the show, isn't it? And then I hear my cue: "Evans. Take the shot."

You, the viewer at home, you don't hear any of that. You hear the target begging and crying, yeah. And you hear the soundtrack swell. But this whole moment, it's crafted by the production team. Everything culminates in this one moment. And as for me, Taylor Evans, my face is projected on a few hundred million screens across the country: taken together, this is an unstoppable force.

BAM.

Like I was saying: it's a reflex. You put a weapon in my hand, and somebody will die.

But here in my condo, halfway to our room, my wife stirs in my arms, withering in her drunkenness. Suddenly, her eyes flutter open. And through a herculean effort, she manages to focus them on me.

"You," Candis says, garbled. "Don't touch me." The color returns to her face: her cheeks first, then her lips. "Don't you fucking touch me," she shouts, pushing out of my arms. She claws and scratches until finally, I let go. Her head smacks hard against the floor and I stand over her, stunned.

A skull fracture. A concussion. *Oh, Candis.*

"You monster," she says, crawling away. "You're a fucking monster."

Then, of all things, I hear the television in the living room, the commentators continuing their conversation.

"Another success," the pundit says. "Another happy ending. All thanks to Taylor Evans. Such dedication, determination. He's an American hero, doing the Lord's work..."

And now I'm angry. Angry that Candis would do this to me. The table next to me, along the wall, I throw it to the ground. The table and all the stupid shit atop crashes to the floor. I kick through the clutter as I leave Candis in the hall — she'll pass out soon enough, and the cleaning bots will nudge her awake in the morning.

Me, I stomp into the bathroom. *I'm Taylor Evans,* I tell myself. Finding my reflection in the mirror, I rip off the sponsor-emblazoned tracksuit, shredding it in the process. It's junk anyway. I'd never wear it again. I grab a towel — custom, expensive, more than you could afford — and turn to the shower.

Next to it is a full-length window, the kind they have in the swankiest of penthouses, and I stop. Bare ass naked, I look myself over in the glass, head to toe. I flex this way and that, my muscles rippling. Me, *I'm Taylor fucking Evans.*

I look beyond my reflection at the city outside, just for comparison's sake. This country, this world, it's barren and dark. It's pathetic. Those people down there — the viewers who love me and those who hate me — they don't have anything like this. My body, my money, my life...

You don't have anything like this.

I rotate my torso, admiring my deltoids, my biceps. People would kill to be me. People would kill to be Taylor Evans. In the shower, I turn the water full blast. I step into the stream. I let the hot mist envelop me.

If you were me, after a day like this, you'd probably be crushed by emotions. But it's nothing I'm not used to. The power. The pressure. The bloodshed. It's all just another day on the job.

You, the day's adrenaline roller coaster would leave you spent and exhausted. But not me. Not Taylor Evans.

Feeling that water on your face, cleansing and pure, you'd probably break down altogether. Your whole psyche would shatter and crumble at the weight of it all. Your whole being, every ounce of yourself, would be praying that the worst of it might be washed away. That it'd be sucked down the drain and be gone for good…

But not me.

Not Taylor Evans.

Somebody like you, somebody raised to believe that violence is bad, somebody who turns in disgust to misogyny, to materialism, somebody appalled at the horror and hopelessness of this unforgiving world, you might clasp your hands over your face, covering the tears, covering your shame and guilt. Because you're weak. Because you're scared.

But you're not Taylor Evans.

Defeated. Destroyed. Somebody like you might lean against the tile wall, your whole body heaving as you sob. Somebody like you, you might slide slowly down, crumbling to the base of the shower, disappearing into the steam. Somebody like you would just disappear from this world. And be gone. So long and goodbye.

But not Taylor Evans. That's not how he's wired. He's a machine. But despite all that, despite me being me…

I mean, who knows? But maybe, the way you would crumble, the way you would cry…

Maybe that is what I do after all.

CHAPTER 3

"Did you fuck her?" he asks. The statement is less of a question and more of closing punctuation. End of conversation. Moving on.

I shrug, then shake my head.

"Then what does it matter?" he continues with finality.

The man before me is Brent Milner. Captain Brent Milner. And he looks at me critically. It's not entirely with disdain. But if you were here, standing in our broadcast-ready training facility on the sixtieth floor of Trucast Tower, you'd probably be backing away from him right now.

Milner doesn't like distractions. And he doesn't like drama. When he has a mission, he completes it. And his mission today, right now, is to keep me as sharp an instrument of murder as possible.

Emotions dull the blade.

"There are two types of hammers," he says, his voice booming in the studio expanse. We are in one of the many training facilities throughout the building. But this one, this is where we spend the most time. "Effective and ineffective," he continues.

This is a mantra I've heard a thousand times before. This is the kind of wisdom Milner spouts regularly. But he waits for me to give him my full attention before he finishes. Reluctantly, I give it to him, and our eyes meet.

"Now you have to choose, Evans," he says. "What kind of hammer are you going to be today?"

"Effective," I say, feeling stupid.

Captain Brent Milner is one of the original hammers, now retired. But he still holds the record for most kills — a record I am on track to shatter.

Regardless, this sixty-something is as imposing today, in his black jumpsuit and gold Rolex, as when he hung up his armor. Standing a few inches taller than me, he remains a brick wall. And the gray five o'clock shadow that perpetually adorns his jaw only accentuates his chiseled features...

More or less, Milner is me in thirty years.

When it comes to retired hammers, they enjoy a life of luxury. Some go on to careers in corporate America, some continue into the entertainment industry, while others go into politics. But as for Milner, he never strayed too far from home. And now, as a network consultant, he's paid handsomely. When he's not on the air providing analysis, he's training the next generation of hammers… and keeping me at the top of my game.

I'll be honest, everything I know I learned from him. But don't think that's earned me any warmth from this man. Milner is the prototypical hammer from the days before we were trained from childhood. Each of us, every hammer, is sliced from him. And today, foolishly, perhaps out of desperation, I asked the man a question. That question was this: what is the difference between a memory and a dream?

Simple, yeah. But stupid. It rolled out of my mouth before I could stop it. Milner glared at me. This question had nothing to do with battlefield awareness or breach maneuvers or whatever. Instead, this was a question about one's abstract inner thoughts. In other words, I asked him about emotions. And that kind of shit, from a hammer, is unacceptable.

Like I said: emotions dull the blade.

Me, I stammered. "There's a woman," I said, blurting it out. But I left it at that.

Milner looked at me, looked down at me. And finally, killing the subject, he asked: "Did you fuck her?"

Was it a memory or a dream? — that was my question.

But Milner was right — *What does it matter?*

Presently, if you were up in the control room overlooking the studio, you'd have a clear vantage of us approaching the center of the facility. We have the whole place to ourselves, and already two dozen rectangular LED television panels are sliding into position, surrounding us. Inactive, these panels look like twelve-foot-tall monoliths. Lifeless and inert.

You see, one of the basic tenets of being a hammer is knowing your maps...

Yeah, maps.

Sure, it doesn't take long for augmented directions to pop up in our heads-up displays, but it's not instant. Consequently, most of a hammer's downtime is spent studying city maps. So, if a target runs on us, you can anticipate their escape and give chase without delay. Any hesitation gives that target ample time to throw us off their trail. So, the solution is old-school and analog: our brains.

To date, no target has successfully evaded the hammer. And on my watch, none ever will. So, yeah, this immersive training exercise positioning itself around us: it's a glorified rat maze that's proven better than virtual reality. This setup is tangible and real. But it's also confusing and disorienting... and that's the point.

Additionally, this facility and the various exercises lend themselves far better to the numerous reality-tv programs chronicling the next generation of hammers. Unlike me, who enjoys private access, the hammers-in-training are pushed through the grinder dozens at a time for dramatic effect. You can find such programming on any of the network's subscription-based platforms.

Milner and I, we step into our respective start-squares — one for the instructor and one for the trainee. Both are marked on the floor. And standing within them, each of us is safe from the moving LED panels.

"St. Louis," Milner says. On command, the panels begin to configure along tracks on the floor. If you were watching from the control room, you'd see them racing by us, seemingly unpredictable in their movements. It's a spectacle, definitely. But that's what the network wants...

Whether you're greeting fans, training, or killing targets: make it a spectacle.

Once in place, the LED panels flicker on, and from my vantage, the illusion is entirely convincing. I now find myself standing alone on a city street. Burned-out cars line the curb, and derelict storefronts cover the block. The effect is to-scale but impressive.

Me, I glance over my shoulder and spot the Gateway Arch, silhouetted by the gloomy night sky. With the Mississippi River between me and the iconic stainless-steel landmark, I immediately know I'm in East St. Louis.

Once a bustling industrial center, this town and the people who live here have been used and abused for nearly a century. And since the last outbreak of national race riots — and the ensuing draconian measures that stamped them out — this, and most neighborhoods like it, are bad places to be, no matter the time of day or whether you have criminal intent or not.

Somewhere along the way, urban renewal simply became martial law. And those stupid enough to protest it, to riot against police brutality or systemic racism or whatever — even vocal critics online — were carted off to re-education camps, some of whom were never seen again.

It's incredible how effectively that cuts down on dissent. Sooner or later, everybody falls into line.

As for that woman, the one I foolishly asked Milner about: no, I didn't fuck her. It wasn't *that* kind of dream. Or memory. Or whatever it was. It's just that this woman, I see her often. In my dreams, I mean. And the dream, it's always the same. But I've been having it more frequently, more vividly.

In this dream, I'm running. But I'm not chasing a target or hunting a criminal. It's not a production or anything like that. In fact, I'm just a kid. Hence why I think it might be a memory, if that's even possible.

Me, in the dream, if I look down, I can see the pill-shaped, velcro-strapped sneakers of a toddler, the corduroy overalls of a child...

So, I'm young. If it's me, I mean.

"Fifth and Missouri," Milner says, hidden in the maze of panels. This, the intersection that Milner has called out, is where my theoretical target is heading; their likely escape route. And I know enough about East St. Louis to understand why: that's a MetroLink station. If the target times it right, they could hop on any number of trains and scatter to the wind.

A few blocks to my left, I spot the old Spivey Building, an East St. Louis relic. The building was once a sign of the community's prosperity — now it's collapsed in on itself. What's left of it is enough to determine my location, though.

Three blocks over, one block down: I'm at the corner of Eighth and MLK. I swivel and dart between a row of LED panels — from my POV, I'm sprinting westward down

Eight Street. Turning right, I cut down to Fifth. The road ends, and I dart through an old park, its playground rusted and forgotten.

In the dream, I'm pretty sure I'm also in a park. It's probably something like this one in East St. Louis, with a swing set and slide and all that. In my dream, though, I trip and fall. My elbows dig into the pavement. The pain is searing, and my tears are hot on my face...

And then, there she is, this woman. Out of nowhere. If this were your dream, you'd think this woman was your mother. You might think she's your grandmother; she has that kind of presence. She's beautiful and strong, and she swoops me in her arms, cradling me.

She looks at my elbow, wipes the dirt and blood away, then kisses the scrape. And just like that, the pain is gone. Relief washes over me, the kid in the dream. She wipes the tears from my cheeks and helps me to my feet. And then we're running, the two of us.

Running and laughing, hand in hand...

And all is good in the world.

Me, I slide into Milner waiting at Fifth and Missouri, the elevated metro station just over his shoulder.

"Very good, Evans," he says, pleased.

A good chase like that, a foot race, the audience loves that shit. It's the kind of spectacle the network loves to give them. A firefight up there on the station: that's gold. Milner and I return to our respective start-squares, and my training continues.

Chicago.

Trenton.

Cincinnati.

At Milner's command, the panels disassemble and reconfigure themselves into the layout of another city, another neighborhood, each a potential target's local stomping grounds. And I know the layouts of all of them. I know all their intricacies.

So, this woman in my dream: maybe you're right. Maybe she is my mother or grandmother. But I don't know; I don't have a clue. Because the thing about memories is this: we're not supposed to have them. Hammers, I mean.

Zero. Nada. Zilch.

As children, we were selected by the network to join the hammer program. Hundreds of us, with dozens more added every year. Like the child Janissaries of the old Ottoman Empire, we were taken from our families and trained to be obedient and loyal soldiers...

It's an honor, an incredible honor, for both the child and the family, trust me.

Through a heavy regiment of psychoanalysis and heavy sedation, all memories and emotions are flushed from our minds, leaving a blank, programmable slate free from guilt and remorse. Sure, emotions and personalities still emerge — we are human, after all — but such traits and quirks have consistently rated high with test audiences. But still...

Milner is the first person I've told about this woman, about these dreams. But his response, his cold indifference, shouldn't surprise me. Unlike us, Milner wasn't raised to be a hammer. Looking at him now, his face is riddled with shrapnel scars from wars past — Milner was a Navy Seal. A disgraced Navy Seal. Whatever war crimes Milner committed, they were barred from publication long ago, deemed too sensitive for public consumption. But this point still resonates with me: the network didn't make Milner into a monster... he already was a monster.

When *The Eagle's Hammer* first went on the air, when the network first cobbled it together, they didn't pluck the finest and brightest that the military had to offer. These proto-hammers weren't top-class graduates from the academies; they weren't celebrated medal recipients. No, those original hammers were war criminals, forever indebted to whichever president pardoned them for this purpose.

At the time, the top military brass was appalled. Those that served with them in combat, they were outraged. But once the killing began, they kept their mouths shut: both soldiers and civilians alike...

Fuller Park.

Central West.

North Fairmount.

Our training continues, with me bouncing all over the country. I'm zoned out, going through the motions — this shit, it comes easy to me. I hear Milner calling out cities. And I find the destination, no problem.

But then I land somewhere unexpected…

Me, I find myself in front of a park. And the familiarity of the location jars me. From my look alone, you might wonder if this is the park from my dream… but it's not. This park is Rittenhouse Square… in Center City, Philadelphia. This is *my* neighborhood. I live here. Slowly I turn to face the gleaming, ultra-modern high-rise behind me.

Up there, in the penthouse, that's my place. I picture my wife helpless in the hall last night. I think of myself in the shower…

What the hell am I doing here?

"Rizzo and eighteenth," Milner says.

Again, I hear him hidden behind the panels. But that address, that's *this* address: where we are now. I turn back to the park, toward Rittenhouse Square. I look left, up through the trees, and spot where Milner and I are currently standing — Trucast Tower. The sight of it repulses me.

"Clock's ticking, Evans," Milner says.

Uncertain, my feet begin moving all on their own — one in front of the other, faster and faster. I rush toward Walnut, then turn down Eighteenth. Block after block blurs by. And then I see him, Milner, waiting for me at the base of the tower, standing in Trucast Plaza, smirking.

"What is this?" I ask, approaching him slowly.

"A good hammer always knows their way home, boy," Milner says, enjoying my discomfort. He steps toward me and pokes me with his finger. "They always find their way home."

CHAPTER 4

"Good," the man says, his voice low. "That's it. Now turn."

My entire life, people have always told me what to do. My earliest memory? Waking up in the co-ed dormitory, maybe nine or ten years old — about the age your kid is now. I woke up, startled by my new surroundings, a drill instructor shouting at us. I was scared and confused, but I caught on quickly. From that moment on, they barked orders, and I obeyed them.

"Look away," the man says now, directing me. "Now at me."

As a kid, their orders began simple and mundane. They started as chores.

Wake up. Brush your teeth. Wash your face.

Good job. Well done. Thatta boy.

But as I got older, they became strange.

The thing is, though, as a kid, I'd become so accustomed to their commands that I barely stopped to reflect on them. I just did them. And did them. And did them. And the people ordering me to do these things, they seemed just as pleased, all the same…

As long as I obeyed, that is.

Slice the calf's throat. Bludgeon the diseased goat. Execute this illegal migrant.

Good job. Well done. Thatta boy.

"Nice," the photographer says, lowering his high-end camera to peer over the lens. In my hand, I hold a fifty-five-pound dumbbell halfway to my shoulder, pumping my bicep to the size of a melon. I can hold this pose, this weight, all day. "Very nice," he adds, feigning interest.

Photo shoots like this are a regular occurrence. The images find their way to the various social media accounts of the network and/or that week's sponsors. When people scroll their feeds, it's my face they see the most. Sort of like Big Brother, except I'm promoting corporate garbage — but pro-tip: be sure to like and share that shit, because they're tracking all that data.

Located on the third floor of Trucast Tower, this gym is used exclusively by us hammers. And I spend hours here.

Lifting this, curling that. All the while, a dozen network assistants fawn over me. To my left and right are full-length mirrors and various exercise machines — typical gym stuff.

In front of me, massive windows overlook the lobby below. Down there, every inch is polished-smooth and translucent. The lobby looks like the future we were always promised: bright, hopeful, and white. Sure, outside this building, the nation and its infrastructure are crumbling ruins. But here, looking down, you'd never guess it. The decor is top-notch, plundered from the finest museums. Everything from Roman columns to Greek sculptures to Brooklyn graffiti is on display. But it's all just ancient history used to prop up the present, the here and now, however flaccid it may actually be.

As I continue my workout, a river of worker bees flows below. These are the nameless, faceless faithful employees of the Trucast Corporation. They don't look at me — their faces buried in their hand terminals — but they know I'm up here.

On a given day, I'll pass by a thousand sets of eyes — men and women whose entire livelihood is based on me and what I do for the network — and not one will even glance at me. But not because I'm irrelevant. Out of fear. These people are scared to death of me.

Can you blame them?

Sometimes I think of the ridiculousness of it all. I think of myself in spandex, pumping, curling, and squatting. All while they scurry to their cubicles to do whatever menial task they've been hired to do, for whatever meager wage keeps them coming. And they do it all despite society telling them — through social media or pop culture — that it's not enough. That raising a family, putting food on the table, paying bills, whatever — it's not enough.

Look. What people have to realize is this: you don't tell us what the American Dream is. We tell you. And if it's six-pack abs, that's what it is. If it's a new car or designer jeans, you better swipe that credit card because you have to have it. You're nothing if you don't. And if it always seems just a bit out of reach; and if you bleed out paying interest striving for it... Well, that's not our problem. That's economics.

My eyes drift toward the far wall of the lobby where video banners loop promos for the network's most popular programs. Within the montage of shows and highlights, I spot my wife Candis perky and smiling. I catch a glimpse of *The Eagle's Hammer* studio anchors welcoming the audience to another execution. There's a moment with Milner doing what he does, paternal and authoritative. And then there's the main attraction: *The Eagle's Hammer*.

Me, I watch myself, decked out in full assault gear, doing what I do: murder people. Even in the promo, they don't shy away from the full brutality of the moment. I pull the trigger, and the target keels over. Then the camera lingers before pushing slowly toward me, all very dramatic. I flip up my helmet's visor and stare at the camera — or you, the viewer at home — with cold, hard eyes.

Me, staring at myself, glaring back at myself, I look away. Beneath me, the mass of people ebbs and flows in time with the array of elevators. They come and go, come and go. It's no wonder they don't look up at me — would you?

And then I see her. Sticking out like a rock in a river, I spot a woman staring back at me, watching me. Our eyes lock, and I'm stunned. This woman, her hair thick and curly, her eyes caramel-colored, she looks right at me, neither fawning over me nor shrinking away in fear. She is calm, her expression an enigma.

I step toward the glass, transfixed.

"Mister Evans," a voice says, seemingly far away. "Mister Evans," the voice repeats, and I turn to find Zack Uchida hovering over my shoulder — did he spot the woman too? "Today's production meeting is in thirty minutes," he says.

Zack's a good kid… or he's just good at kissing ass. Ten years my junior, he's been my assistant for three. Punctual and put together, he's a company man through and through. He probably believes everything the network tells him, probably has since birth. Every generation is more brainwashed than the last, after all.

But I trust him, which might be foolish of me. He's a network hack, after all. Have I ever told him this? Have I ever confided in him? Hell no. Have I ever conversed with him in any capacity other than professional? No way. But that woman, she pops back into my mind.

"Zack," I say, catching him off guard — this may be the first word I've spoken to him in weeks. "Who is that?" I ask, gesturing toward the lobby.

But when I peer down through the glass, she's gone.

Zack forces a laugh — he may be terrified of me. He steps next to me and gazes out. But instead of searching the faces below, looking for that women's soft, lightly freckled features, he focuses on that enormous video banner across the way. His eyes lock on the looping network promo, on the footage of me killing another hapless target. Me on-screen, I turn toward the camera and flip up my visor…

"That's you," Zack says wistfully. "Taylor Evans."

The American Dream.

CHAPTER 5

Taylor Evans scans the bedroom, his gun held at arm's length. In the closet, watching him, the terrified children cry uncontrollably. But the hammer's target — the woman accused of committing whatever crime most convenient for that night's broadcast — she's not in here.

She's not in the closet, or under the bed, or hiding behind the door. So, Evans and the team move on, kicking in every door along the hallway. Finally, one door remains. The bathroom — *it's always the bathroom.*

But Evans, as if suddenly struck with stupidity, makes to move on. Or perhaps, somehow, he's decided to show mercy on the poor soul inside. Then he hesitates. Evans turns back, his eyes locked on the door...

And the image freezes on-screen.

"Good," a voice says. It's the voice of Blake Riley, producer/director of our nightly broadcast. "The audience knows where she is. You know where she is. But this, this is suspense."

Me, I look from myself paused on-screen to Riley. Meeting my gaze, he nods. "Nice work, Evans," he says.

Me and the other five hammers, we're seated at a long table centered in a pool of light — this is our daily production meeting. Riley, wearing a trendy but casual sports jacket and jeans, stands before the multitiered conference room. The hammers and I, and the entire production staff, are reviewing last night's show. Just outside the table, sitting silently on the periphery, are the assistants and technical crew, ordered from most to least important.

Riley gestures, and the video resumes. On-screen, Taylor Evans backtracks to the remaining door.

"Good," Riley says, watching along. "You're waiting for the hover-cams to get into position. Very good." Riley checks a tablet in his hand. "Ratings peaked here, by the way," he adds, glancing back at the table. "The audience loves this shit."

On-screen, the other hammers fall into place around Evans.

"Hitting your marks," Riley says, nodding his satisfaction. "Good. Good."

On-screen, the suspense builds. Evans grits his teeth as if he's about to give the command to kick down the door. But in reality, the other hammers and I were waiting for Riley's cue in our earpieces. It all looks organic and natural on the big screen, though. But just as the music reaches its crescendo, one of the other hammers steps into the shot, blocking the camera's view.

Riley pauses the video, frustrated. "Dammit, Blair," he says, casting his gaze at the hammers seated at the table. "Don't block his camera. Don't block Evans' camera. Jesus Christ. How hard is this to understand?"

Blair, the youngest of the hammers, turns red with embarrassment. The whole room is staring at him. He's new to this, with only a dozen episodes under his belt. He's an up-and-comer, to be sure. But he lacks *the special something* that makes a hammer stand out from the rest.

Blair and the rest of the hammer team, they sit across from me at the table. And I hate to even mention them. I hate to even think of them. The five of them, they mean nothing to me. And I mean nothing to them...

Well, that's not exactly true. I do mean something to them: I'm the competition. Having come up through the same intense education/training program as me, the hammers know I'm the top dog. But that doesn't mean I'm invincible. If it guaranteed a spot in the limelight, any one of them would happily slit my throat. Loyalty means nothing — except to the network itself.

Seated next to Blair are Gorman and Samra. They're dangerous, competent men. They shed all the jitters and nerves that Blair still exhibits long ago. Gorman and Samra are good-looking guys too. They're quiet and calculated, but that doesn't make them any less dangerous.

Sitting further down the table, like Tweedle Dee and Tweedle Dumb, are Riggs and CJ. This pair should make you very uncomfortable. Sometimes lovers, occasional rivals, they're never far apart. Riggs is stunning, but she's an unsheathed knife: dangerous and unpredictable.

CJ, the brute, he's my likely successor. He's got the look and intensity. The only thing standing in his way is me. I have seniority over all of them. And they hate me for it. That's the thing about hammers: we're supposed to hate each other. The competition between us, even as children, was so intense that it wasn't uncommon for kids to snuff each other out — yeah, even as children. Horrific, sure — but it makes for some damn good television. The more ruthless, the more relatable to the viewers at home.

Riley, our producer, turns back toward the screen. He gestures, and the video resumes at double speed. Riley's overseen the production for several years now. He wasn't my first producer; that was Joaquin Rogers. Joaquin saw over me as I transitioned from clueless rookie to team leader. He was why America fell in love with me. The way he ran things, it was different. It wasn't so much about the blood and gore. It wasn't so much about terrorizing the viewers at home. But Joaquin, he's gone now.

And as they say, the show must go on.

Sure, I miss the guy. Maybe he felt like an ally in all this, somebody I could call a friend. Perhaps he'd look at me and see through the facade. Maybe when I'd get back from a kill, he'd place a reassuring hand on my shoulder and squeeze. The kind of display that tells a young, clueless rookie literally washing blood from his hands that it's okay. Everything was going to be okay. But he's gone. Now, Riley is calling the shots. And that's that…

Emotions dull the blade.

On-screen, Taylor Evans kicks down the bathroom door. The team enters and finds the target hiding behind the shower curtain. Evans levels his weapon. He pulls the trigger…

Riley pauses the video with me standing over the target's now lifeless body. If you were here, you might look away from the gore, the blood and brains on the bathroom tiles. You might storm out of the room in shock and disgust. But here in the conference room, dozens of people sit motionless, each silently convincing themselves that this is acceptable.

"Good. Good. Good," Riley says, pleased. "All in all, a good show." The people around me nod in agreement, but I stare at myself on-screen — at Taylor Evans.

"Great job, bro," a voice whispers to me. It's Silas Hansen. You might remember him as one of the news anchors at the start of the broadcast. He's a nasty son of a bitch, with a cocky grin permanently affixed to his face. Seated next to him is Skylar O'Brien, the female anchor. She's a striking woman, but her perpetual, untreated anxiety overshadows her personality. She notices my gaze and forces a smile.

Filling in the rest of the table are a plethora of also-rans and network pundits. Getting a chance to sit at the table with the 'grownups' makes them all harder than hell. But also seated with us is Milner, his chin propped up in his hand, bored.

Riley turns to him, offering him the floor. "Captain Milner," he says. "Any notes?"

Milner clears his throat and stands. If you thought he was scary before, you should see him in a three-piece, wide lapel suit. Eyeing me — and only me — he begins: "Bloodier. Make it bloodier."

As he walks around the table, everyone swivels in their chair to follow him, afraid to take their eyes off him. Then he stops behind Skylar — the anchorwoman. From where I sit, I watch her shift uncomfortably, craning her neck toward Milner behind her.

"Last night, Evans," Milner says, "you put the gun to her head like this. Angled down."

He steps up to Skylar and puts an imaginary gun to her head. Skylar gasps nervously. Then forces a smile — this is a privilege, after all. Milner, he doesn't bat an eye at her discomfort. Instead, he glares at me.

"Angled down," he repeats forcefully. "See?"

I nod ever so slightly — this is all Hammer Training 101.

"You have to angle up," Milner says, startling Skylar. He grabs the back of her head and repositions his imaginary gun, jabbing his fingers into her forehead. Skylar, her eyes are now clenched shut. She's terrified.

"Bam," Milner shouts, pulling the trigger. The room watches him wide-eyed. "Blow her brains up," he says, shoving Skylar away. "Cover everything." His hands mimic an explosion of gore spraying into the air. "People never forget seeing brains dripping off the ceiling, Evans. Give it to them."

As Milner eyes me, I wonder how much he misses killing people. Finally, I respectfully nod, and the room relaxes as Milner returns to his seat.

Skylar rubs the streaks of eyeliner from her cheeks and shrugs it off with a laugh. If she wasn't such a heartless bitch on television, you might feel bad for her.

"Thank you, Captain," Riley says, returning to his spot front and center. "Now, moving on. Here's the rundown on tonight's target."

With a swipe of his fingers, he flings an image from his tablet to the big screen. The image is a profile picture plucked from social media. It's a photo of a twenty-something young woman. In the photo, she's dressed up and smiling. But she won't be smiling tonight. Not when we bust down her door.

The woman's location catches my eye: Philadelphia. We're staying home tonight.

"Fishtown," Riley says, specifying an almost forgotten neighborhood northeast of downtown. The other hammers sound their dismay.

"Gonna need a strong disinfectant," Riggs says, cackling at her own joke. She's referring to the recent outbreak that wreaked havoc on the impoverished community. The poor don't get vaccines, not anymore. A few others seated at the table force a laugh — but it's not funny, not really.

The other hammers and I, we scan the rest of the intel on display — it's pretty standard stuff.

"Ration hoarding?" Samra asks, disappointed. "Seriously?"

Riley shrugs. "It's a capital offense," he says. "The law's the law."

On-screen, the presentation splits into four sections. One is an overhead map of the target's neighborhood. Another is the layout of the target's apartment. The third is a computer-animated POV rendering, detailing what each of us is likely to see: the front stoop, the stairs to the second floor, the target's front door. And the fourth is a pre-visualization of the production itself — this is how we learn tonight's scenes and blocking.

We see the show exactly how they want it to go down. Every second, every move, every word we mutter, it's all planned out in advance. Any deviation from that plan is unacceptable, and punishment can be severe — the less thinking on our part, the better.

Yeah, it's stupid simple — it's simple to the lowest common denominator (Blair.) Each of us, each hammer, is represented by a tiny cartoon avatar with our face mapped on it. We sit here and watch. And then tonight, all we need to do is repeat what our avatar does now. It's that stupid.

"As always," Riley says, "your orders are to eliminate the target. And all associates…"

*All associate*s, I muse. That's a new one. But more blood equals better ratings.

On-screen, the avatars arrive at the target's location along their street. Each hammer jumps out of their hammermobile and converges on the sidewalk. Together, they enter the premises. Gorman takes the lead up the stairs, followed by CJ and the others. We get to the door, and my avatar steps forward and knocks. There's no answer — we always knock, but there's never an answer. Then Blair kicks in the door — typical rookie duty.

While all this is happening, my eyes slide to the apartment's layout. The front door opens to a foyer; the living room is to the left, and a doorway leads to the kitchen — pretty basic stuff. A few windows here and there, but there's little chance of escape. And if they did, I'd put my money on them running for the Interstate 95 expressway, just down the block.

On-screen, our little avatars enter the home. We sweep the rooms and approach the bathroom — it's always the bathroom.

"So, who gets the kill?" Riggs asks, impatient.

Like I told you, each hammer dreams of the spotlight: the big kill. Riggs, her mouth is watering at the thought of taking the lead for once, undoubtedly lusting for the fame that would follow. But it'll never be her. As I said, it's CJ who's number two. He's put in his time, and he's got the scars. By now, you'd think CJ and I would have developed some sort of camaraderie. But trust me, there's none. CJ would just as happily put a slug between my eyes as the target's — especially if it makes him the lead hammer.

Riley clears his throat, a nervous tic when he's uncomfortable. And I can feel CJ staring at me. "The kill goes to Evans," Riley says.

The team collectively groans.

"Again?" Gorman asks.

"This really is the Taylor Evans show, ain't it?" Riggs asks.

"How about spreading the wealth?" Samra asks.

Riley shrugs. "Hey. Not my decision," he says. "Orders are orders." He looks at me and repeats himself. "Evans, you get the kill." Riley glances at the others. "Now, the rest of you," he says. "Why don't you shut the fuck up? We have work to do."

Me, I can feel CJ glaring at me, burning a hole in my back. He has every right to be fuming mad. He's put his time in; he deserves some glory. But on the other hand, he can go fuck himself.

"We're sending the details to your tablets," Riley says. "All the intel on the target and location, it's there. Study it. Know it. As always, this shit's confidential. So, no spoilers, alright?" He looks about the room, then nods his satisfaction. "Call-time is eighteen hundred. We're live at twenty hundred."

"Prime-fucking-time," Riggs says under her breath.

With the meeting adjourned, the staff quickly clears out. There's no sense being around us bloodthirsty monsters any longer than necessary. I stay seated, ignoring the searing gaze of the other hammers. But out of the corner of my eye, I spot her: the woman from the lobby.

She, too, remains seated and is looking my way.

Me, I freeze as if any movement might scare her off.

"Zack," I say, whispering to my assistant over my shoulder. He's seated just behind me, his head buried in his hand terminal. "Zack," I repeat, snapping my fingers. "Who is that?"

Zack looks up, bewildered. "Who?" he asks. Flustered, he scans the crowd. Unlike last time, he spots her. But as soon as we both look her way, the woman stands. She slides a bag over her shoulder, then heads for the exit. Zack and I, we stare like idiots as, just before leaving, she glances back at me.

"I have no idea, sir," Zack says, perplexed. "I've never seen her before."

Me, I consider this. But it doesn't seem right. New staff members don't just pop up overnight. "Do me a favor," I say to Zack, pulling him close. "Find out."

Zack blinks, then nods. "Yes, sir."

He stands, grabs his things, then heads to the door.

Me, I'm still sitting when I notice Milner eyeing me. Pushing himself up from the table, he hovers toward me. Before he even opens his mouth, I know what he's going to say…

"The Eight-Four, Evans. Let's go."

CHAPTER 6

Tell me, what do you know of the Nuremberg Trials? You
don't hear much of them these days, not since fascism
swung back into fashion. But for me, the less I know about
myself, the more I embrace history. There are lessons to be
learned, no matter how forgotten they may be.

As for the Nuremberg Trials, they were a series of military tribunals following the Second World War in which top
German officials were prosecuted for their crimes against
humanity. In fact, that term — *crimes against humanity* —
that's where that comes from. Those on trial were the crème
de la crème of the German war machine. They were the
ones who planned and executed the Final Solution, aka the

Holocaust, aka the mass murder of seven million
European Jews.

These people were terrifying, yeah. They were heartless,
soulless, and vile. But it's important to remember: these
people were people. Flesh and blood, like you and me.
And yet, they did what they did. There's a lesson there. It's
not monsters that commit horrible deeds; it's people. It's
always people.

People like Milner and me… and Hanna Hernandez.

The express elevator slows to a stop, and the doors open
to the Eight-Four. Whenever I step off the elevator into
this stark white foyer, I think of Joaquin Rogers, our old
producer/director. Glancing at Milner, I bet he does too.

As I said, Joaquin ran the show when I got promoted
to the team, my big break. Grey-haired and pleasant, he
had a calming quality about him. And I think it's fair to say
that just about all of us respected the guy — he certainly
respected each of us. But that day, up here on the Eight-
Four, none of us dared move a muscle when Hernandez
took a blade to his stomach and gutted him.

Hernandez, she made us all watch. She wanted to prove
a point: that her word was law, and disobedience would
be punished harshly. Me, I'd seen hundreds of people die
before that day — but none that I'd ever cared for. Not
wanting to witness the scene and unsure where to look, I

focused on the blood pooling on the white tile floor beneath his body, fully aware of how much Hernandez enjoyed the kill, the ecstasy it brought her.

Even Milner looked away, eventually.

Joaquin's crime was simple: he cut away from the gore. Instead of showing the gruesome details, he'd linger on me instead. He'd let the viewers look away. And he did this against Hernandez's wishes. Americans, Joaquin said, didn't need more violence in their lives.

Hernandez thought otherwise.

The next day, all evidence that Joaquin Rogers existed was scrubbed from the company's directories. Even emails would bounce back undelivered. His family, his husband, and kids: who knows what happened to them? They all disappeared…

Me, I watched the blood soak into his blazer, then never spoke of it again.

Now, as Milner and I approach the office, a weapon detection system scans us, not that there are any guards up here — Hernandez doesn't believe in them. Guards are for politicians and celebrities. Hernandez welcomes violence; it's her religion. To her, it's a dog-eat-dog world out there. And, if one would be foolish enough to come after her: she'd be all too happy to cut out your heart and eat it in front of you.

The system chimes nonetheless, and Milner and I are free to enter. Getting summoned up here isn't unusual, not for me — I'm the network's pride and joy, after all. But it's like trekking to the top of Mount Olympus to visit Zeus himself. Here in the mortal realm, though, Zeus goes by the name Hanna Hernandez. And instead of being the king of gods, she's the Trucast Corporation's top CEO.

Let me explain just how large and influential the Trucast Corporation is. Imagine a company completely unchecked by government oversight or regulations. Imagine this company is the world's largest internet provider, the country's mightiest media conglomerate, and, thanks to numerous acquisitions — most of them hostile — the leading manufacturer of personal mobile devices.

And now, for you at home, imagine this company has a complete record of all your online activity: every transaction, every internet search, every text and email you've ever sent or received. And imagine that company has stored all that data, just in case it proves valuable in the future.

That kind of blackmail material, that goes for everybody, too: even the President of the United States, whose voice I hear wafting from Hernandez's office. The president, his name is Jordan Norton. That the company has him in their pocket goes without saying. Obnoxious and self-serving, he'd lick Hernandez's heels if she wanted him to. If he'd ever dare meet her in person, that is.

Now I'm not saying that the Trucast Corporation rules the world: that would be ridiculous. There are even a few individuals wealthier than Hernandez — the ultra-elite. But between them and the four other global mega-corporations, the Trucast Corporation holds the most cards out of the deck.

The others, run by their own oligarchs, they control real estate, energy, and capital. And since humanity is forever tied to these industries, whoever controls them has a seat at the table. But what the Trucast Corporation has above all the others is perception. They manipulate how the public sees their world; they control how the people think. You see, if the Trucast Corporation tells the people that they're content, then they're content. And if they tell them they're unhappy, then they're unhappy. It's as simple as that.

And that's precisely why President Norton calls in to wish Hanna Hernandez a good day, every day. As for Norton, I'm not even sure how many terms he's served, nor care. Politics was never my thing, and the presidency just isn't what it used to be. In fact, it's more like a prison sentence than an honor. Assassination attempts became so commonplace that the National Guard has the president always on the move. Utilizing the nation's old rail system —

largely abandoned since the death of manufacturing in the
country — he's locked up in an elaborate rail car designed
to resemble the old Oval Office… before it was nuked, that
is. So, the president, he can be anywhere at any time. I hear
there are even decoy trains out there on the rails.

Stepping into the office, Milner and I spot Hernandez
at her glass-topped desk. Her designer suit is gun-metal
gray, which contrasts nicely with her white, radiating hair.
Hanna Hernandez is a presence on par with history's greats:
Alexander III of Macedon, Genghis Khan of the Mongol
Empire, Napoleon Bonaparte, Emperor of France… you get
the idea. She projects complete authority and control. But
there is a coldness about her. One could easily mistake it
for arrogance. But it's more than that, as if all of us — me,
Milner, the president — we are mere pawns at her disposal,
participants in a game too large to comprehend.

Here at the Trucast Corporation, it is her vision that we
deliver. But let me point out that, by the very nature of the
corporate structure, there is a board of directors above her.
But they wouldn't dare cross her lest she makes it a personal
matter. This woman, she is powerful. Powerful enough to
have the president himself — his bloated face plastered on
a video screen across from her — check in daily, eager for
marching orders.

Even before Washington D.C. was wiped out, it was clear the United States was a failed republic. By then, the country had devolved into an illiberal dumpster fire. And climate change, global pandemics, and hopeless income inequality all proved to be accelerants. Desperate to curb what was known as *Fake News*, the Trucast Corporation became the only government-endorsed media outlet. And since the Trucast Corporation was also the world's leading internet provider, all other news outlets found their bandwidth choked down to nil — all with the federal government's blessing, of course.

But the Trucast Corporation ran with this power. Before long, the politicians who unleashed it fell into line. What public outrage there was — traditionalists who preached the Constitution and the importance of a free and independent press — was brushed aside, then ignored... and finally, hammered.

Was the network pumping out propaganda? Certainly. Were they bending the nation to its will? Absolutely. But instead of state-run media, it became a media-run state — the tail began wagging the dog.

Milner and I, we approach Hernandez's desk. While the president rambles on about his latest cultural grievances, she spots us. Raising a finger, she silences the man mid-sentence.

"Mister Evans," she says, greeting me with a smile. As for Milner, she doesn't even glance his way.

"Is that Evans?" Norton asks, peering around the edges of his monitor. I step into his field of view, and he chortles — even he's star-struck. "Hell of a good show last night, son."

"Thank you, sir," I say.

The president sizes me up and lowers his voice. "Tell me, son," he says with a sadistic grin. "What's it like?"

Milner and I, we exchange a knowing glance — the elite love this question. The sanctioned murder we are entitled to is a fetish of theirs. Me, I play coy.

"What's that, sir?" I ask.

"You know what I'm talking about," the president says. He scoots closer to his camera until his face fills the entire screen. "What's it like pulling that trigger, huh? That woman, the girl from last night…" The president, he licks his lips — he's practically drooling. "What's it like?"

"Mister Evans is here to discuss tonight's production, Mister President," Hernandez says, growing impatient.

"Of course," Norton says, chuckling. "Well, I'll be watching, son. Don't let me down now, ya hear?" I nod. But the president lunges again toward his camera. "I bet you like it, don't you? Her on her knees, begging. I bet you love it…"

With a quick gesture, Hernandez ends the video call. Mercifully, the president's face disappears, and the monitor retracts into the ceiling.

"What an insufferable son of a bitch," Hernandez says, flippant. Standing up, she motions toward a furniture arrangement overlooking the city. Predictably, a staggeringly expensive bottle of champagne sits on the table, chilling in a bucket of ice, two crystal flutes at the ready. "Evans," she says. "Join me."

Leading me toward the sofa, she gazes back at Milner and shakes her head. Milner stops in his tracks — he's not invited. Hesitant, he watches me continue with her before turning back toward the elevator. As I sit, I watch him exit, dejected — the errand boy is no longer needed.

Hernandez sits, then slides close to me. "How are you, Taylor?" she asks — few people call me by my first name.

"Good, ma'am," I say.

"And Candis?" she asks — it was Hernandez who introduced us a decade ago. I picture my wife on the floor of our condo, passed out.

"Good, ma'am," I say.

"Mhmm," Hernandez says, looking me over. She reaches up and runs her fingers through my hair. The gesture is both tender and yet possessive. I am the product, after all. If you were here, being groomed by Hernandez, you'd be holding your breath. You'd be so scared you wouldn't dare move a muscle. You wouldn't even blink.

The thing about Hernandez that scares people the most are the stories. There are so many stories. Some involve greedy prima donnas who tried to force a pay raise out of her. There are stories of desperate employees — victims of the toxic, masochistic culture that permeates the company — coming to her for help. Some stories include fools who turned down an offer, not knowing they didn't have a choice. But these stories all end the same way.

People like this — people that cross Hernandez — these people disappear. They're dragged up to the helipad, and the network helicopter takes them for a flight. Only, when these people go up, they don't come back down — not in the helicopter at least. They're tossed out somewhere over New Jersey, splattering in some abandoned shopping mall or elementary school parking lot. And Hernandez, she even goes for the ride.

That moment when somebody realizes their life is about to end, at your hands no less, that's a thrill. Pulling the trigger on national television or giving your goons the final nod of approval, it's a thrill. And Hernandez is more addicted to it than me.

These people, they fall to their deaths. Their bodies pulverize on impact, and nobody cares to look up their dental records. Their families, even after their loved ones have gone missing, they don't say shit. They don't call the authorities or make a stink. They don't even dare have a funeral service… lest the hammer pays them a visit.

That's Hanna Hernandez for you. That's the woman running her fingers through my hair.

"Taylor, my little janissary," she says with a self-satisfied little smile. "You mean so much to this country. The people look up to you. They aspire to be you. And that's why I summoned you up here today. Because they need you — I need you — more than ever." She places a hand on my leg. "Tonight needs to be special, Taylor."

She stands up and walks to the window, peering at the city below. "I'm going to tell you something, something that can't leave this room. Understand?" She glances at me, and I nod. "The president," she says, rolling her eyes. "The little shit's scared. And he has good reason to be." She returns to the couch, leaning on the armrest. "The ratings. They're lower than ever."

I blink. How can that be? Every American is forced to watch. Their devices scan and register their identities. Punishment for refusing is severe. The ratings and retention rates, they're not about selling commercial time. They're about control. If one is stupid enough to defy the mandate and not watch the program, one runs the risk of the nats showing up at your door. You and your family get dragged off for reeducation. Or worse yet, the hammer stops by. And that's that.

"I'm afraid it's true," Hernandez says, reading my thoughts. "The less they watch, the less control we have over their lives. And the less control we have, the more likely they are to question authority. And you know where that goes. It ends in bloodshed. It always does." Hernandez sighs. "We don't want that," she says, despondent.

I consider this. I consider that the public might not be watching. That would mean only one thing: the people aren't scared anymore. And If they're not scared...

The thing about Americans is that they've always held the Constitution dear to their hearts. And they always will. But it's like the Bible in every hotel room. What good is it actually doing anybody?

Now, don't get me wrong: Hernandez didn't make things this way. Nor did President Norton or any of his predecessors. Our society's monoculture shattered over a century ago. Democracy was nothing but a corpse after that. It was inevitable that the body would fall off the horse. And it was equally inevitable that another rider would saddle up. That rider was the Trucast Corporation. And now it's Hanna Hernandez with the reins in her hands.

Keeping you watching is paramount to everything we do here at the network. As Hernandez said, it prevents bloodshed. Without the constant pressure of fear, a genuine uprising of the underclasses might manifest. And we can't have that. But that's the brilliance of *The Eagle's Hammer*. It is that fear. Its class warfare spun to its purest form. Sure, there are nightly human sacrifices. But those sacrifices keep people in line, preventing hundreds of more deaths. Maybe even thousands. And isn't that a good thing?

But if the ratings are dropping, viewers have become desensitized. And there's only one way to fix that...

I feel Hernandez watching me. For her, violence is always the answer. And dialing it up is the best way — perhaps the only way — to keep the people in line. That's why she killed Joaquin Rogers; that was the lesson we all learned.

My eyes, they fall to the white tile floor.

"Tell me, Taylor," she says, reaching for the champagne. "Have we lost them? Have we lost the people?"

Me, I shake my head. "Never, ma'am," I say.

She nods. "You're a true patriot," she says, pleased. She pours the champagne into the two flutes, then hands me one. Without thinking, I take it from her. "The more we terrify them, the happier their lives. We do this for them, you know. For the greater good."

She sits down again, sliding close. She holds out her crystal flute toward me.

"We have to set an example tonight," she says, her eyes locked on mine. "They look up to you, the people. You lead them by example. That's why I want you to send them a message. To every viewer glued to our broadcast, yeah. But also to every viewer not watching. I want it loud enough that they hear it too." She leans toward me. "Listen, Evans," she says — switching to my last name. "Let me be clear: I'm asking you to dial it up tonight. I'm asking you to hammer hard. I want you to send a message and send it loud. Do you understand?"

I nod, and her face relaxes. She takes my free hand in hers, and I think of the blade she had that day, the day she killed Joaquin. Instead of my hand, she held the handle of that knife. One weapon is traded for another. I know my place in her world...

"You'll do that for me?" she asks, smiling again.

"Of course," I say. We clink the crystal in our hands, then sip at the bubbly champagne.

What choice do I have?

CHAPTER 7

I stare at her, stunned. Here she is again, the woman —
black, curly hair, caramel-colored eyes. And a look that says
she couldn't care less about me.

As I'm about to step off the high-speed rail that has
brought us to the Eagle's Nest, I find her among the dozen
production assistants greeting me and the other hammers.
I've never seen this woman before today. And now I'm
seeing her everywhere. The other hammers, they step
around me irritably. The woman, she turns to lead the
group down the first of a series of corridors.

Me, I have no choice but to follow.

This tunnel is about twenty feet wide and a hundred
feet long, with patriotic music playing softly from hidden

speakers. Back in the day, this was an underground bunker deep beneath the Air Force base. Top military brass was to be rushed down here in the event of an all-out war. Since then, the corridor has been painted flat black, and the flickering fluorescent lights are now cool-blue LEDs. The look is modern and sleek. But the air is still musty and damp.

Whatever equipment originally adorned these walls has long since been stripped away, replaced with video screens, one after another. Specific screens are dedicated to individual team members with our best, most violent highlights playing on loop. It doesn't take long to learn where one can see themselves in action, shifting one's attention from one screen to the next, never missing a beat.

We're cattle, for sure. We're simpletons easily distracted by our own visage — it doesn't matter what we're doing as long as we look good doing it. But not me, not today.

Instead, I'm watching this woman strutting ahead of me. I'm studying how her hair falls on her shoulders and the curve of her hips, and I'm reminded of Hanna Hernandez — of that woman's confidence. This woman here, deep in this dungeon, she has that same energy, like she owns the place.

Now, you might be wondering: if our target lives in Philadelphia, what the hell are we doing here in the middle of New Jersey? And the answer is simple: spectacle.

Even if we are just going to blast off right back to Philly, we go through these motions. We gear up like soldiers heading to war. Then launch into the sky, burning a couple hundred thousand dollars' worth of jet fuel for one reason: spectacle.

It's what the audience wants.

And it's what the network gives them.

Mounted on the tunnel walls are rows of remote cameras tracking us. For an exuberant fee, you can subscribe to all-access coverage. Even the Eagle's Nest isn't off-limits. So, if watching CJ take a massive shit is your thing. Or watching Riggs pick the blood from her nails piques your interest; well, this is for you.

The hammers and I, ushered along by the staff, file into the first prep station. Each of these rooms serves a specific purpose. This is the pharmacy. And a PPE-wearing nurse-tech greets each hammer with a giant syringe in hand. Just at the sight of the needle, my mouth is already watering. Jabbed into my arm, I feel the benefits immediately.

Amphetamine. Dextroamphetamine. Methamphetamine. Whatever this shit is, I feel it surge through me. I can see clearer, think faster, and breathe deeper. Instantly, I am smarter, sexier, stronger — and more than ready for tonight's slaying.

My fists and teeth clenched, I look back at the woman. She's following along, checking off a list on her hand terminal as we proceed. From what I can tell, she appears to know what she's doing. Glancing at the other hammers and staff, nobody else seems to notice her.

They herd us into the next room: the locker room. Here we find our digs for this evening's production. Undressing, I pull off today's sponsored tracksuit and eye the woman in my mirror. Despite my lack of clothing, she avoids my gaze, not even glancing in my direction. Rude.

Pulling on my attire — my body armor, kevlar vest, and hard-knuckle gloves; everything black, everything tactical — I suit up and strap in. It's hard not to fall into character, to not get excited about what's coming. Once finished, we look badass, and we know it. Admiring our reflections, we savor the image. Embroidered above our hearts is *The Eagle's Hammer* logo. Beautiful.

Then we're off to the final room: the armory. We each have an assortment of personalized weapons laid out for us and a technician eager to help. Me, I look over today's offering: a set of submachine guns, light enough to carry one in each hand. Dramatic, yeah. But no accuracy. Not my style. I move on to my choice of large, over-the-top bull-pup-style assault rifles. Not bad. Any of these will do. And, of course, polished and waiting: my trusted Colt/Detonics hybrid handgun...

This gun has killed a lot of people.

I pick up and cradle the weapon in my hand. Palming the handle, a light on the barrel toggles to green — this weapon, it's ready to kill. Only assigned users can use their designated weapons. This goes for all our gear. Our biosignatures are scanned and identified — thus preventing a target from grabbing one of our guns in desperation.

I holster it and slide spare magazines into my belt.

Next, the technician carefully picks up my helmet. Placing it atop my head, she tests its fit and then secures it. Flicking the visor down activates a sophisticated heads-up display system, and numerous readouts and augmented reality info are presented to me. The technician — and any other potential targets — are automatically identified, complete with their most recent social media posts, height and weight, address, and pre-existing medical conditions. Shellfish allergy... too bad.

I immediately turn toward the mystery woman, and an attractive profile pic pops up with her name and address. Patrisse Flynn. Yeah, she looks like a Patrisse. As for her home address: Kensington. Another rundown neighborhood of Philly, but aren't they all? Her employment info scrolls up: production assistant, Trucast Corporation. Yeah, that's a given. But I'm provided the duration of her employment as well: three years.

Three years? How am I just noticing her now? I return to her details scrolling in my HUD — five foot ten, hundred and thirty-seven pounds — and her eyes dart toward me as if she knows what I'm doing, that I'm online stalking her. If it wasn't for my blackened visor, our eyes might have met. Instead, she stares at her reflection, brushes her bangs from her eyes, and turns away.

Meanwhile, my technician watches me expectantly. I give her a thumbs-up: shit's working.

A freight elevator takes us and our entourage toward the surface. And as we wait, I glance at the other hammers. Quiet and focused, with their assault rifles clutched to their chests, muzzles down, I wonder what's going through each of their heads. We all want something, I remind myself. Knowing a rival's wants and needs allows one to anticipate their actions. So, what do they want?

Blair, the rookie: he's just a kid. He wants respect. But it's the one thing he doesn't get.

Samra: he's a believer. Having drank the Kool-Aid long ago, he's the only one of us that's convinced we're making the world a better place.

Gorman: he's the smart one. He's well aware of the financial opportunities presented to hammers, both in service and in retirement. He knows it's all a game, but he plays it well.

Riggs. Riggs is an interesting one. Her moral compass points her toward anarchy. She'd be happy watching the world burn. But what she wants most is CJ. Not in a lovey-dovey way, but in the materialistic, objective way. She wants to own him.

CJ, on the other hand, what he wants is simple: he wants me out of the way. He wants to be top dog, the alpha. But as long as I'm here, he'll always be a second-stringer. That's just how it works.

But as for myself, what do I want?

Now that I'm here on the elevator, at the cusp of another mission, drugged and buzzing, everything that's come before seems like a blur. Killing our target last night, assaulting my wife at home, even Hernandez's plea this afternoon: they all seem like distant memories. Even the woman in my dream seems irrelevant now. Even the fact that I mentioned her to Milner no longer bothers me.

Me, I'm just locked and loaded and ready to kill.

The freight elevator jerks to a stop, and the doors open. Waiting for us in the hangar is the Eagle itself: a converted military scramjet deployment vehicle. Roughly the size of an old commercial airliner, the plane is jet-black and angular, with its only markings being *The Eagle's Hammer* logo and the USA flag. Approaching it, we probably look like vintage NASA astronauts about to board a rocket. But instead of inspiring hope and optimism, we are servants of death herself.

We enter the jet via a ramp into the cargo bay. Here, each of our hammermobiles awaits us, parked front to back and stacked upon girders and ramps. My car sits front and center, always in the lead. Teams of technicians buzz about, checking and double-checking that the two dozen hover units hanging from the walls like sleeping bats are ready and secure.

Me, I step up to my hammermobile, and another red/green permission light toggles green, granting me access. Without touching it, the automated car door unlatches and swings open. I climb into the cockpit and look over the assortment of flashing idiot lights — they're all for show. I have no idea what any of them mean. Here in my vehicle, I have another moment to myself, and I immediately think of the woman vexing me: Patrisse Flynn.

What does a woman like that want?

Candis, my wife: she wants money and possessions. She wants the lifestyle she's busy selling to her viewers. Hanna Hernandez: she wants power and control of everybody and everything. But this woman, Patrisse Flynn, she is an enigma. She neither fears me nor desires me. Hell, she didn't even bat an eye as I changed clothes in front of her. Again: rude.

The other hammers and I, Candis and Hernandez — and Milner too — we are all ruthless. We're selfish and self-serving because that is how they want us to be. That is how they want us all to be because that makes us good consumers, which makes us easy to control.

So why do I not see that same cruelty in Patrisse Flynn?

A pair of technicians crawl into the car with me, fastening and checking my harness. In my helmet, magnets latch onto my seat's headrest, securing my neck for the insane acceleration/deceleration my body is about to endure. Meanwhile, a weapons tech stows my assault rifle within reach.

Sitting there, I hear the lead mechanic approach, his prosthetic leg clanking on the ramp as he walks. He pauses to gaze at me through the windshield, and my HUD reminds me of his name: Anton Williams. This guy's been here as long as I have. And these cars — the hammermobiles — they're his pride and joy.

Pulling my straps nice and tight, the techs clear out of my vehicle, and Williams steps to my door, shutting it. He kneels carefully at my window, and I know all he can see is his own reflection in my visor. Nevertheless, the guy leans in and gestures for me to lift it.

I don't know why, but I do it.

Williams smiles. "You know, Evans," he says, shouting over the rumble of the scramjet's idling engines. "This car, it doesn't have to run in autonomous mode. You can have some fun with it."

Me, I blink. Nobody drives anymore; nobody wants to. Sure, every hammer has had extensive pursuit training behind the wheel. But the thought of actually driving an automobile, that's beneath me. And to think that this man just asked me that... I see red.

"Why the hell would I want to do that?" I snap.

Williams laughs. He raises his hands in mock surrender.

"I'm just saying. You might like taking control of things, that's all," he says.

I glance at the steering wheel, the dials, the blinking lights. All of it frustrates me.

"You don't think I'm in control?" I ask. "Fuck off."

I flip my visor back down and reach toward my assault rifle. Placing my hand on its handle, I'm immediately soothed. Williams takes the hint and moves on, amused with himself. That limp of his, it's because he likes to take risks. Well, one of those risks caught up to him. And he lost a leg because of it. If he keeps this up with me, he'll lose more than a leg.

Far away, a klaxon sounds. All the hammers are in place and strapped in. The support staff scurries off the jet — the asshole lead mechanic as well. Take-off is imminent, and I'm relieved. Relieved to be doing what I'm meant to do. No more thinking. Only doing.

In front of me, I watch the ramp close and seal. An ominous red safety light fills the void. In my helmet, the program-feed appears in my visor, and my earpiece crackles to life.

The entire jet lurches forward. I can't see any of it, but we're taxing onto the tarmac. In my ear, I hear the crew back in the control room, back in Trucast Tower. I feel their excitement just as I feel the jet's engines throttling up.

Baker Riley, the producer, he's barking orders, getting the studio talent in position. I can picture them, all of them, in place and waiting.

"*Ready in ten. Nine,*" Riley says in my ear, to the entire staff and crew. With the scramjet about to launch, the broadcast is poised to begin.

Hanna Hernandez, I picture her watching from the Eight-Four with one eye on her video screen and the other on the broadcast's real-time ratings...

"*Eight. Seven.*"

Milner, I know he's in the studio, standing just off set, waiting for his expertise to be called upon. But I know he's fuming — back in the day, he'd have had the one-on-one with Hernandez in her office. Now he's her glorified staff assistant, and he's bitter about it...

"*Six. Five.*"

Somewhere out there is my wife, drunk and high and tapped out already.

"*Four. Three.*"

And then there's you. You probably just got home from work: tired, underpaid, and exhausted. You probably just fed the kid, helped him with his homework, and all that. But this whole evening, you were dreading the moment your hand terminal would buzz — the moment everybody's terminals buzz, and all of America is obligated to watch...

"*Two...*"

Your kid, he's already sprinting to the living room, sliding to his knees as the video screen automatically changes stations to the network's broadcast. And you, you're sick to your stomach as you enter the room. You eye your husband as you join him on the couch. And with that one look, you share the unspoken truth, the unspoken horror: it's showtime.

"*One...*"

But me, at the head of it all, I'm only thinking about one thing, one person...

Patrisse Flynn.

CHAPTER 8

The lights fade up in the studio as the afterburners ignite, launching the scramjet down the runway. Within seconds, the plane is airborne and pulling 9 Gs — enough to knock out the most hardened fighter pilots.

"Crime is out of control," Skylar O'Brien says to her camera, her makeup now perfect.

"Sins are being committed," Silas Hansen says, his hair slicked back.

"And our children are in danger," Skylar adds.

At ninety-thousand feet already, the turbojets cut out, and the hypersonic scramjet engines ignite. As the vehicle accelerates past Mach 6, the sonic boom rattles windows along much of the East coast — if people didn't know we were on-the-air, they do now.

In the control room, Baker Riley stands before the monitor wall, each screen a different camera source. This program is his canvas; the cameras are his paints. With them, he will craft this story.

"Ready camera two," he says. "And... take," he says, snapping his fingers. The program cuts to the two-shot with Silas and Skylar seated side by side at the anchor desk.

"But rest easy, America," Silas says, suddenly reassuring.

"Because *The Eagle's Hammer*," Skylar says, all smiles.

"Is about to drop," they say together, triumphant.

Outside, the nose of the scramjet is glowing red-hot from air friction. At this speed, it'd only take a half-hour to fly to the UCC — the United Commonwealths of California. There, *The Eagle's Hammer* program is banned; even watching it can garner hefty fines. There, we're accused of being mass murderers and monsters. But that's no surprise.

Even before Washington D.C. was wiped out, the country was fractured beyond repair. Texas had already seceded, and many southern states were on the brink. But after D.C., there was no hope of pulling it back together. On the east coast, martial law became the norm, but many on the west coast resisted. Once California called it quits, the rest of their neighbors followed suit. But if the mega-corporations could still siphon their profits despite the new borders, what difference did it really make?

So off California went, drafting a new constitution and declaring their independence. Out west, elections still matter, the courts aren't owned, and justice prevails — all things once taken for granted here back east. But now, all this is presented as just another outrage for the network to sell its viewers. For years, people demanded war. But that war never came.

Already, the scramjet begins its descent. Its destination: the Philadelphia Airport, another long-abandoned relic from a more prosperous economic past.

You, you're in your living room watching. Your kid, he's beyond excited. With his Taylor Evans action figure clutched to his chest, he bounces up and down on the carpet. This program is his drug. But he's not the only addict — millions of people are glued to their video screens. A lot of them are lustful for the impending bloodshed. But most of them, they're people like you: people quietly praying that tonight is not their night, that the hammer isn't coming for them.

The scramjet's landing gear connects with the tarmac and the vehicle slams on its brakes. The cargo bay door swings open and thuds against the pavement. The hammermobiles unlatch as the ramp descends and the hover-cams zip outside, maneuvering into position…

You, your heart skips a beat when you recognize the city skyline: Philadelphia. You reflexively reach for your husband's hand… *Oh no.*

The hammermobiles launch down the ramp one after another. They turn toward the city and charge ahead, the cameras chasing after them — it's all very choreographed and cool. The music is up-tempo and driving.

You, you're holding your breath, panicking as you watch us race up Interstate 95. To our right: the Delaware River and New Jersey beyond that. You glance at your husband, and for a moment — just a flicker of time — you wonder if he's turned you in. And what's even more sickening is that you know, with absolute certainty, that he's thinking the same thing about you.

In your head, the faces of neighbors and associates flash by. Fuck, it could be anybody. Friends, coworkers, second cousins — it could be absolutely anybody. This is how we keep you, all of you, in line: by hammering away until you're too afraid to think for yourself…

Traffic clears out of our way as we race below underpasses and charge over overpasses. Half-abandoned neighborhoods, empty storefronts, and collapsed warehouses: it's all a blur as the team approaches Fishtown.

We take an offramp and blow through a red light, indifferent to the pedestrians fleeing for their lives. Another block, and the team fish-tails around a corner. We cross beneath the freeway and enter a quiet, low-income neighborhood. Single-family row homes and ugly apartment blocks line the street, all in various levels of decrepitude.

You, you watch the team screech to a stop. Dozens of residents are already peeking out their windows, the live broadcast flickering on their televisions behind them. But relief washes over you. This isn't your neighborhood; we're not coming for you after all.

You're so relieved that you forget that a human being is about to die. You forget that moments ago, paranoia overtook you. Your husband, your friends, and coworkers: you suspected them all. Now, you're so thankful that you can't help but crack a smile; the stark horror of this world suddenly doesn't seem so bad — and that's a sentiment shared by just about everybody who doesn't live on that street.

This is your drug: the high of survival. And that's the addictive nature of *The Eagle's Hammer*: one moment's terror is another moment's joy. All is well, as long as it isn't you. But then your son's enthusiasm jars you back to reality, dragging you into the horror you're so eager to escape.

"Let's bust 'em," your kid says — yeah, that's my catchphrase out of his mouth. He beat me to the punch.

On your television, the hammers exit their cars and join at the curb. You watch me unholster my gun and stare up at the building as my camera positions itself. And then I say the line myself: "Let's bust 'em."

Your kid screams ecstatically.

On-screen, Blair charges up to the building's front door, kicking it right off its hinges. Gun drawn, Samra dramatically clears the lobby, swinging his carbine from one corner to the other.

"Clear," he shouts, and the other hammers and I pour inside, staying in formation. With stained tiles and flickering fluorescent lights, the lobby is disgusting. But it doesn't faze us in the least. As scripted, Gorman takes the lead up the dingy stairs. A hover-cam tracks behind him, giving the audience a POV view over his shoulder.

"Great start," Riley says in our ears. "Looking good."

Me, I'm running up the stairs two at a time. In my head, I'm going through all the motions for when we reach the target's landing. I'm not thinking about anything except hitting my marks and nailing my blocking.

With all of us in position, the cameras hover into place. I step up to the door and pretend to listen to what's on the other side. Then I knock.

"*The Eagle's Hammer*," I say. "Open up." — but they never do. Exchanging glances with CJ and Riggs, I step aside. Blair positions himself in front of the door and, on my cue, kicks it in. The lock snaps, and the door slams open.

You, you watch me peek in and then step inside, gun drawn. I scan the living room, ignoring the television tuned in to tonight's broadcast — though my quarter-profile looks good, damn good. This is all pretty standard stuff, repeated nightly. The way I think of it: I'm a feather in the breeze. Like a monkey shot into space, this is what I've been trained to do.

Do I regret being a hammer? That would be like regretting being born. America would be nothing without us. A lawless, anarchist dumpster fire. Without us, there'd be no hope. We are this nation's salvation.

You, you're watching your kid watch me. Me, I find our target cowering behind her couch. The cameras surround us as she stands up, her hands raised in surrender. The woman is short, her hair frazzled. Everything's going according to plan, adhering perfectly to the script, when the target, she looks me in the eyes...

Brave. Very brave. She's the third woman to look me in the eyes today.

"Please," she says. And for some reason, through all the commotion around me and in my earpiece — the whir of the drone's propellers, Riley barking directions at the crew — I hear her, my target. "Please don't hurt them, my babies. All they are is hungry…"

Them? I scan the room beyond her and spot who she's referring to, her accomplices. Behind her are a half dozen children, an assortment of ages and ethnicities that she's taken in as her own.

"Please don't hurt them," she says.

Kill all accomplices — those were our orders at the production meeting. *Don't let me down* — that's what Hernandez made me promise in her office.

I can see myself doing it; I can visualize it all: me pulling the trigger. The muzzle flashes. The loud cracks. One. Two. Three. I level off at the others, their stunned, flushed white faces staring back at me. Four. Five. Six. Riggs laughing maniacally.

I'm Taylor Evans; I can do anything. Just do it and go home, I think. I turn toward the woman. The other hammers, the hover-cameras, they're all in position around me, growing impatient.

You, you're watching me.

Your kid, he's watching me.

"Please," the target sobs. "All they are is hungry." But for me, my thoughts are a million miles away. I can hear the after-show praise already: history in the making — record-breaking ratings. I can see Hernandez sitting on her desk, her legs crossed, that smile on her face and a champagne flute in hand. *Taylor Evans: American Hero.*

"You're a monster," Candis will say, clawing at me to stay away from her.

"God bless Taylor Evans," a late-night studio pundit will say.

"Did you fuck her?" Milner will ask. But instead of my wife or the woman in my dreams, I think of Patrisse Flynn...

And I snap back to here and now, tonight's target cowering in front of me. I hope this Patrisse Flynn is watching, I muse, leveling my trusted Colt/Detonics hybrid. On the handgun's barrel, the permissions-light toggles green. All systems go.

"Very nice pacing," Riley says in my ear. "Take your time. Wait for the camera."

Me, I know you're watching. I know you're all watching. But staring down the barrel of my gun at the target, I think of her...

Patrisse Flynn... I hope she's watching.

"You look great, Evans," Riley says. "Take the shot."

My finger tightens on the trigger. The target shuts her eyes. Clearly, this is not how she imagined her life would end. Clearly, she never expected to be slaughtered on live television, her children huddled and crying behind her...

But this is America.

"Evans," Riley says, stern. "Take the shot."

Me, I'm ready. You put a weapon in my hand, and this is what I do...

"Evans," Riley says, growing frustrated.

Me, I know Hernandez is watching. I know Milner is watching. I know the whole country is watching, their eyes glued to the broadcast. And I know what they want...

"Evans," Riley says, now terse. "Take the fucking shot."

Me, I hope Patrisse Flynn is watching...

"No," I say.

CHAPTER 9

At first, it seems like a glitch. You can't quite believe your ears. Maybe it was a mistake, a misunderstanding. Or perhaps Taylor Evans simply misspoke. But deep down, you and your family know exactly what I said.

Back in the control room, I can picture Riley and the staff; in the studio, I can see Silas and Skylar: all of them stunned. I hear their awkward silence and feel their uneasy glances. Somebody somewhere whispers to a colleague the question everybody has on their mind: "What did he say?"

Up on the Eight-Four, I can feel Hernandez's seething rage. And here, in the target's apartment, surrounded by the other hammers and network cameras, I can feel the pressure of a billion unblinking eyeballs watching me with bated breath.

I don't know why I just said what I said. But I said it.

The target, she blinks, then backs away in bewilderment. Even the children — the starving, defenseless children — they're no longer crying. Even they stare at me, dumbfounded.

In my ear, Riley clears his throat, that nervous tic of his. "Evans," he says, trying to stay cool and calm. "Take the shot."

Me, I know where I am. I know what I'm supposed to do. But all I can think of is…

Patrisse Flynn.

"No," I say.

Eyeing me, the other hammers shift uncomfortably in their body armor. I hear Riley cover his microphone with his palm and ask somebody in the control room: "He can't do that, can he? Say no?"

His question is meant with silence.

Me and the other hammers, we're all thinking the same thing: disobeying an Eagle's order is a capital offense, punishable by death. What always seemed like an empty and unnecessary threat to keep us disciplined and loyal suddenly takes on new precedence.

Back in the control room, the phone rings. I hear Riley reluctantly answer it. "Hello," he says, his voice now quivering. It's Hanna Hernandez, no doubt. "Yes, ma'am," he says, solemn. He sets the receiver down and turns back toward the broadcast.

"Hammers," Riley says, his mouth dry. "Execute Taylor Evans…"

The other hammers glance at each other. This command — an order from Hanna Hernandez herself, no less — is a dream come true. Riggs can't help but crack a smile. CJ, he's all too happy to oblige the order. The target, the children, they're already scrambling for cover.

"Evans," CJ says, swinging his rifle toward me. "I never did like you."

Patrisse Flynn. I hope she's watching.

At that moment, all my gear powers down. My weapons disarm, and my visor goes dark. And for the first time in my life, I'm helpless… except for my training.

No more thinking, only doing.

Before CJ can pull his trigger, I rip my helmet off and throw it so hard and fast into his stupid face that his visor cracks. His head snaps back, and he stumbles into the others. Swinging my now non-functional assault rifle off my shoulder, I bat Riggs' weapon out of her hands, snapping a few of her fingers in the process.

She shrieks in pain and coils away. But I grab her, then use her as a shield. The other hammers, just as they're about to cut me down in a hail of bullets, they're rendered impotent. They lower their carbines, frustrated. Their orders were to kill me — not Riggs. So, I drag her kicking and screaming toward the kitchen.

The hammers watch as I turn a corner and exit their line of sight. Backing into the counter, I glance about, desperate to find something, anything to give me an advantage. Then I spot it: the microwave. Opening the appliance, I toss my handgun inside and mash the keypad. The timer starts, the microwave lights up, and the gun begins to rotate.

"Evans," Riggs says, clutching my forearm against her throat. "You're a real son of a bitch."

The other hammers burst into the kitchen right on cue. Inside the microwave, bolts of electricity pop and flash. And then the gunpowder ignites…

BOOM.

Hot shrapnel knocks us to the floor and blows out the kitchen light. Me, I'm stunned, my ears ringing. Without my helmet, I can't see shit, but I sense the other hammers stirring around me. Outside, a light-unit sweeps the window, casting its floodlight through the now-shattered glass.

I know I only have seconds to escape, but how? Another tenet of *The Eagle's Hammer* that's repeatedly drilled into our heads: when no options are good options, choose the least bad option…

The window. I sprint for it and smash through the glass. Launching myself into the air, I grab hold of the light-unit. The drone bucks from my weight and then plummets forward into the building. The light-unit and I crumble and fall, landing hard in the back alley. Finding my face against the pavement, I spring to my feet. A sharp pain stabs at my ankle — I have my limits, and a two-story leap was pushing my luck.

What now? Where do I go? What do I do?

Don't think, do.

I scramble for a filthy, rusty dumpster as the hammers open fire from above. The alley is devastated. Bullets rain down, ricocheting off the pavement and pounding the brickwork behind me. There's a break in the barrage. Peeking through a bullet hole torn in the dumpster, I spot Riggs and CJ leaning out the window.

"Don't be an asshole, Evans," Riggs shouts, the drones hovering hesitant and unsure between us. "You know the law."

They step back into the kitchen, out of view. Me, I glance toward the street. Already, a secondary swarm of drones is positioning itself, waiting for me to flee the alley.

Up at the window, I can make out the hammers huddled inside: a production meeting, no doubt — new assignments being doled out. Moments later, Blair leaps out of the window. The rookie lands gracefully and rolls into a crouching position. Not bad, I think.

"You can't run, Evans," Blair says, beaming — this is it, his big shot. He swings his carbine in my direction, savoring the attention — then opens fire.

I duck behind the dumpster, knowing I've got to make my next move. Blair empties his clip, ejects it, and slams another in place.

"Be a man, Evans," he says. "When the hammer drops, there's nowhere to hide. There's nowhere to run."

Me, I shake my head — I hate rookies. I peer down the alley and eye the hammermobiles. With their bulletproof fenders, they'll make good cover.

Blair falls silent as he listens to Riley in his earpiece. If I pay close enough attention, I might be able to hear what they're telling him, what they have up their sleeve. But it doesn't take a genius to figure it out...

Blair unhooks a grenade from his vest — grenades are one of Blair's go-to weapons. Sure, they're woefully ineffective — more flash grenade than explosive — but they look cool. I peek over the dumpster and spot him pulling the pin. With his attention affixed to the nearest hover-cam, the kid isn't even looking at me when he tosses it my way.

I watch the grenade arc through the air. But before it lands, I'm sprinting for the street. The grenade lands in the dumpster, a good toss. Then promptly explodes…

KA-BOOM.

The dumpster rips apart like tin foil. Shielding himself from the blast, Blair eyes the fireball as it rises into the air. Me, I'm leaping over the nearest hammermobile when he snaps from his daze.

"Shit," he says, frustrated. He opens fire.

I slide across the hood just as the salvo arrives. But the armor plating does its job, keeping me alive — for now. The drones, they reposition themselves around me. Glancing over the fender, I see Blair taking his sweet-ass time following me — the network's already dragging this out. Ratings must be through the roof.

"This ends only one way, Evans," Blair says. "With you in a body bag."

Good God. Is all of our dialogue this trite? Cringing, I scramble to the next car. Then the next. But a barrage of bullets pins me down.

As I sit there, bullets and drones whizzing overhead, I spot tonight's target burst out of her apartment building with the kids in tow. The target, she spots me crouched low to the ground, and our eyes meet. And this woman, she gives me a look of appreciation...

She thinks I saved her life.

And I suppose I did.

Blair stops to reload, and the woman and her kids scurry away. Me, I dart to the next vehicle. This one, it's my hammermobile. I leap over the hood, landing behind the car just as Blair opens fire. Keeping low, I slide along the fender. And as I pass the driver's door, I inadvertently come close enough that the vehicle automatically scans me...

To my surprise, the access light toggles green. I pause and stare wide-eyed at the car handle. It shouldn't have unlocked... but Blair is gaining on me.

Don't think, move.

I swing open the door and climb inside. Blair spots me, but his bullets ricochet harmlessly against the bullet-proof plating. Over the violent din, I hear Riley screaming from my car's production radio: "How the fuck did he get in that car?"

I look at the dashboard and all the flashing idiot lights anew. Without a preprogrammed destination, I will have to switch the vehicle to manual, but finding an ignition switch is proving challenging enough. I think of Anton Williams, the mechanic back at the Eagle's Nest — he must be laughing his ass off.

Finally, I spot it: a big round button. I jab at it, and the car powers up.

Blair is now in a full sprint; frustration and panic are smeared across his face. My chances of escape — of actually outrunning *The Eagle's Hammer* — have just improved dramatically. I know it. He knows it. The whole production team knows it.

Pulling another grenade, Blair lobs it at me. Me, I smash the accelerator pedal to the floor, and my hammer-mobile launches from the curb. But Blair's throw is perfect: the grenade thuds against my hood...

BOOM.

The explosion shatters my windshield and jerks the wheel out of my hand. But skidding to a stop, I find the motor still running and ready. Dazed, I spot Blair grinning at me through the spidered glass.

"If he wants a car chase, give him a car chase," Riley crackles on my car's radio.

Blair hurries to his hammermobile, jumps in, and fires it up. We stare at each other, our electric motors fake-rumbling as the hover-units circle overhead...

This is some damn good television.

Cut to a close-up of Blair: this is his big moment. This is the kind of spectacle that the network lives for. Blair, he looks good. Confident and bold. America's holding its breath, waiting for his next move. So, what does Blair do?

He pulls another grenade and lowers his window. Holding it out toward me, letting me see it, he revs his motor.

Me, I roll my eyes. But my attention shifts from Blair's cheap theatrics to the industrial riverfront beyond the freeway overpass. The river offers an unexpected escape possibility…

Blair slams his accelerator. I punch mine. We charge straight toward each other, the camera-units panning to follow the action. It's a good old fashion game of chicken. But at the last moment, Blair flinches. He pulls his grenade back into his car just as we make contact, scrapping fenders before careening apart. But the impact jars him, and he drops the grenade inside his vehicle. It bounces off the seat, then rolls to the floor.

Me, I watch him in my side mirror, swerving wildly.

Desperate to grab the grenade — and not accustomed to manual driving — Blair fails to slow down. Just as he's about to grab the explosive, his vehicle jumps the curb and crashes into a light post. The impact spins the car, then rolls it over onto its roof. Inside, the grenade bounces around like a pinball until the vehicle settles, flipped and thoroughly wrecked. Even the camera drones seem stunned by how fast the action played out.

Blair, still strapped in his seat, eyes the grenade now lying on the vehicle's ceiling. He reaches for it... but it's just out of reach.

"I can't..." Blair's panicked voice squawks on my radio. "I can't reach..."

KA-BOOM.

The grenade explodes. The hammermobile's armor absorbs most of the blast, but inside, Blair is splattered. Blood and guts are everywhere.

Back in the control room, Riley and the production crew watch in horror as a hammer dies during a broadcast for the first time in history. Pouring out onto the street with the other hammers, CJ shakes his head, irritated.

"Amateur," he says. "How fucking amateur."

Me, I floor the accelerator. CJ and the other hammers, they open fire. But it's futile. Their bullets bounce harmlessly off my car as I charge beneath the freeway toward the river. Glancing in my mirror, I spot the hover-units chasing me.

Without letting up, I plow through a chain-link fence, dragging it behind me as I cross an abandoned lot. Then I ramp the sloped floodwall, launching the car into the air.

After a moment of weightlessness, the vehicle corkscrews down and splashes into the river — dark, cold water bursts through the shattered windshield.

Upside down and disoriented, my world goes black.

You, you're watching at home. This — what you just witnessed — is beyond comprehension. Something like this: it just doesn't happen.

Your kid, he turns to you, confused.

"Mom?" he asks.

But you're speechless. With your eyes fixed on the television, you watch as my hammermobile dips beneath the water's surface. A moment later, it disappears altogether, sinking into the deep. And me with it.

The program cuts abruptly back to the studio. Silas and Skylar stare at their camera, white as ghosts. "We now return," Silas says, trembling, "to our regularly scheduled program…"

CHAPTER 10

The sky is a misty blue. And even with tears in his eyes, the kid can spot the puffy clouds above. The woman, he senses her before he sees her. And then, there she is in front of him, smelling of jasmine and oranges. Her jewelry jingles around her wrists as she bends down to him, her necklace gently tapping him on the nose as she wraps him in her warm embrace.

"Now, now," she says, her voice gentle and soft. "Everything's okay. Everything's alright."

Me, my hand shoots up out of the river and grabs the first rung of a rusty ladder. Pulling myself up and out of the water, I glance back at the search party circling the area

where my car sank. Looking for my body, no doubt —
they're desperate to confirm the kill.

The river's current carried me far and fast, which is
good: it gives me time to think. I look toward the city and
spot Trucast Tower. Lighting up the night sky, its reflection
in the water seemingly points right at me as if saying, 'There
he is.' It's an illusion, of course. But I think of Hernandez
atop that building, perched on the Eight-Four. And I think
of Milner by her side.

They will come looking for me.

The water drains out of my clothing as I climb onto
the dock. A dozen sets of dull, tired eyes are staring at me:
vagabonds huddled around burning oil drums. It was these
flickering flames that drew my attention to this abandoned
port. Most of it has been reclaimed by the rising water
levels — no one cared to invest in floodwalls on this side
of the river. These people live among the empty shipping
containers littered about. I'm not sure why they haven't
been rounded up and sent to the work camps down south.
In due time, I suppose.

I'll be honest: these people, they disgust me. But I'm
dangerously close to hypothermia. Shivering uncontrollably, I stumble toward their fire regardless. Watching me
approach, they clear a spot at one of the drums.

I'd expect more fear out of them — I'd expect them to scurry away like cockroaches. Could it be that these people don't know who I am? Does *The Eagle's Hammer* logo on my chest mean nothing to them?

I step up and warm my hands on the flames. If you were here, you'd be throwing yourself into this fire, it's so cold. Me, I'm sizing up my options when I hear the heavy thwap, thwap, thwap of helicopter blades.

I glance back toward the city. As the birthplace of American democracy, it's only fitting that Philadelphia would also be its grave. So, what went wrong? The same things that always wreck empires: ignorance, arrogance, misinformation, and indifference. Those were the magic ingredients that vanquished the pharaohs, humbled Rome, and crumbled the Aztecs. Why would we be any different?

Loose nukes. That's what they called them; that was the stake through the heart. When Texas decided to secede, the first thing the governor did was overrun the military bases within the state's borders. He wanted the fighter jets and weaponry for himself, believing conflict was inevitable. Command and control broke down in the ensuing melee, and a few nuclear weapons went missing. How they got into the hands of the backwoods Michigan militia is anybody's guess, but Washington was there one moment, then gone the next. Nothing was the same after that.

It's important to remember that nothing is inevitable, whether that be prosperity or decline. The difference between one and the other is a million different decisions made by a million individuals. To participate or not. To resist or not. To fight or not. If enough people do nothing, anything can happen.

"Looks like you could use a friend," a voice says.

I turn to find a figure approaching the fire. Judging by his stature and gait, this guy has a military background. Here to challenge me, perhaps? To defend his territory? But when he steps into the light, he greets me with a smile. In his hands is a dry blanket.

"Who are you?" I ask, suspicious.

"A friend," he says, offering me the blanket.

I consider the likely scenarios of how this interaction may play out. He might have somebody hidden in the dark, covering me with a rifle. He could have a knife folded in that blanket, waiting for me to take the bait.

Despite my hesitation, the guy pushes the blanket into my hand. And I find it to be a blanket, nothing more. Still shivering, I wrap it over my shoulders.

Across the river, a helicopter breaks off from the search party and heads this way. Attracted by these fires, no doubt. The first spotlight sweeps the area, and the homeless scatter and hide. Me and this guy, we're left sticking out like a sore thumb. Unsure, I start to back away. But I have no idea where to go or what to do...

"If you run," the man says, "they'll spot you." I eye him, but he's right. "Come with me instead," he says, gesturing to follow him. He takes a few steps toward a nearby shipping container turned on its side. One of its doors lays flat on the ground, open; the other hangs down, obscuring its interior.

Me, I don't move an inch.

"It's your ass, man," the guy says, shrugging. He ducks inside the container and disappears. He's right. That copter is equipped with military-grade tracking equipment — infrared facial recognition sensors, bio-identity scanners, etc. If I run — if I'm singled out and alone — they'll identify me from a mile away. But if I clump with others, I muddy my signal.

I duck into the container, pulling the blanket over my head as the man steps in front of me. Our heat signatures will still read as two individuals, but it should be enough to keep them from identifying me.

The helicopter swoops in, fast and low. Its spotlight sweeps back and forth, and I realize there's about triple the number of people here than I realized — this mob could have easily torn me apart with their bare hands had they wanted to.

The rotor's powerful downwash blows out each fire and blasts apart the cardboard shanties. Then, seemingly content, the helicopter pulls up and heads south along the river.

The man turns to me. "Let's go," he says.

He steps toward the back of the shipping container. Sliding aside a sheet of plywood, he reveals a blow-torched hole in the bottom of the floor. The hole leads down through the pavement and into the ground, complete with a ladder disappearing into the void, which he mounts and descends.

I inch toward the hole and peer down, seeing nothing. Then a flashlight clicks on, its beam shining in my face.

"Come on," the guy says, waving me down.

I look up and out of the container, back toward the river. I watch the helicopters and drones still buzzing about in the distance, then peer back into the hole. It smells — I bet this is a sewer full of human waste dumping into the river. But given my options, following this guy is the least bad.

I climb down, the man illuminating the rungs until I step off into the knee-deep runoff. My suspicions were correct: this sewer is disgusting. If you were here, you'd probably be heaving at this point.

Two other strangers flick on LED headlamps, revealing themselves in the dark. I can't see their faces, but I can see their weapons: carbines, both of them. I size them up, quickly planning how to defend myself. At this close of range, I doubt they'd use the guns lest they risk cutting down their own.

"Relax," my friend says, placing his hand on my chest. "They won't bite." He turns to the two newcomers. "Lead the way."

They obediently turn and trudge up the sewer. The guy, my buddy, he follows suit, and I find myself standing in the dark, the water and debris floating by my ankles.

Again, I consider my options.

And again, this is the least bad option.

I follow the group cautiously, careful not to trip on unseen bulwarks or pipes. After a while, I begin to trust their confidence down here, which allows my thoughts to wander. I replay tonight's action in my head over and over. The target cowering before me, my gun aimed between her eyes. My hesitation, my defiance. Blair's grisly but clumsy death — a hammer has never been killed on live television before. So that's a pretty big first.

As for you at home, I don't think you'll get much sleep tonight. I doubt anybody will. Hernandez, Milner, Silas, and Skylar. My wife and the assistants. The rest of the staff.

Nobody's going to sleep well, especially not knowing what tomorrow will bring.

Was it worth it?

Was *what* worth it?

All I did was make a decision. And since then, that's all I've been doing. I jumped out of that window. I hopped in my car. I drove into the river. Now here I am, following these thugs to who knows where...

But what about Patrisse Flynn?

How does she fit into this?

As we walk, additional soldiers emerge from the shadows. At every cross tunnel, another pair is waiting for us. As their lights sweep their faces, I see an eclectic mix: male, female, non-binary. Black, white, brown. Before long, there's a small army leading the way, escorting me like a prisoner.

Eying their gear, it's outdated but decent. The fatigues they're wearing are tattered and mismatched. But the team seems well-trained and disciplined, minding their corners and staying in formation. All eyes are on point, with their fingers on their triggers, ready for anything. Occasionally, they whisper jokes to each other, cracking smiles or flashing grins. A few times, I catch them glaring back at me. From what I can tell, they're not happy about this assignment, but they're obedient.

What is shocking, though, is that a militia like this shouldn't exist. Not beneath New Jersey, at least. As I said, it was a militia that destroyed D.C. and flushed this nation down the toilet. So, who are these people? And who's calling the shots? I glance ahead at my buddy, curious if he's in command. Nobody's saluted him, but there's respect.

Hours go by, but we keep walking. There's no more talking, no more chit-chat, but the further we go — we must be well east of Camden by now — the more at ease the group seems. Up above, the sun must be rising.

Me, I'm cold and hungry. But I know things can get worse and fast, so I follow along. Turning this way and that, we march on, almost hypnotically. At some point, I realize that despite all my training in maps and city grids, I am completely lost. And maybe that's the point — to deceive and confuse me until I have no clue where I am, nor have any idea how to get back.

Turning one last corner, we're greeted by the dim light of early dawn. The tunnel opens to a drainage ditch, where a continuous trickle of water feeds into the mud. In the light, I see these soldiers for who they are: a tired, haggard group of misfits, malnourished and unconfident.

My buddy, he waits for me at the opening. The others, they stand idly by as I step up and peer out. A warehouse stands before us, located within a seemingly abandoned industrial park. Tattered tarps cover the opening to the sewer, and salvaged wood boards serve as a crude bridge through the mud, leading to the structure. Scanning the horizon, I don't recognize anything — we must be deep in New Jersey.

The other soldiers hop down and head toward the warehouse. As I'm about to follow, the guy, my buddy, raises his hand and stops me.

"Keep that blanket over your head," he says. He points skyward. "Your friends back at the network, they're always watching."

I glance up and deduce he's referring to high-altitude drones. "Where are we?" I ask.

The man grins, then hops down to the bridge.

"We're home," he says.

CHAPTER 11

Rain patters on the mud around us as we approach the entrance. Inside, I hear the murmur of activity: machinery, music, voices, laughter. I stare out from beneath my blanket at the large warehouse. *How can this be?*

We step inside, and the armed soldiers that escorted me here disperse. There are no guards, no security, no nothing. It's just me and my buddy, who smirks at my bewilderment: there are people here. Dozens of them, maybe a hundred.

They shouldn't be here — *this* shouldn't be here.

The network has spent decades convincing us that it wasn't safe outside the cities. But here, in some forgotten industrial tract of New Jersey, I'm in the midst of a seemingly thriving off-grid community.

"How about a tour, man?" the guy asks.

All I can manage is a shrug, and we walk deeper into the complex. Plywood, corrugated plastic, aluminum siding: decades of discarded trash have been repurposed to make walls and barriers, splitting the building into distinct sections. Floodlights hang from the scaffolding, power cables crisscross over us, and a massive skylight has been white-washed at the center of the complex, casting an even, diffused light upon it all.

Rooms are filled with bunk beds, and the mattresses are lined with personal belongings. We pass a health clinic where volunteers tend to the sick and elderly. A library overflows with old and weathered books — most of which are banned, I'm sure. And finally, a cafeteria. The volunteer staff happily serving steaming-hot food.

A cup of hot coffee is handed to me, and I stare at it, shocked — everyone that we pass, everyone we come across, they all just smile at me as if they've never seen me before…

Me, Taylor Evans.

This complex, its very existence, is an abomination. It goes against everything our nation stands for. Why would they — the network, the nats — allow this to exist? Communal living? Free of consumer materialism and corporate culture? A drone strike could take it all out. Call it a gas explosion; blame our nation's crumbling infrastructure...

"Daddy," a child screeches, rushing toward us. The kid runs full speed into the guy's legs, clinging to him.

I blink, stunned. A child? His child?

"Hey buddy," the guy says, kneeling to his son's height. "I want you to meet somebody. This is Mister Evans. He's a friend of mine."

The kid peers up at me. "My name's Jamal, Jamal Culver. And this is my daddy." He hugs the guy again, then seems to consider something, crunching his nose as he thinks. Coming to some sort of decision, he approaches me. About five or six years old, the kid is somewhat disheveled and dirty but healthy and bright-eyed. His clothes are small, bordering on rags, but a neon-colored fanny pack is strapped around his waist. Gauging the kid's eyes, his nose — yeah, I can see the similarities to his father.

"Mister, come here," the kid says, waving me down. "I want to show you something."

I glance at his father, and he shrugs. I don't know many kids. Actually, I don't know any kids. But I oblige him and kneel. The kid zips open his fanny pack and pulls out action figures.

"These're my superheroes," Jamal says. Holding the toys delicately in his fingers, he presents them to me one at a time, rotating them so I can admire them from all sides.

The toys themselves are decades old. The characters' once saturated and bright colors are long-worn away, revealing more of the yellow-molded plastic beneath it than anything. The logos on the characters' chests are barely recognizable, and most are missing fingers; some don't have noses. Despite being dug up from a midden, they are clearly the kid's most prized possessions.

"Impressive," I say. The kid nods, then zips them back up. I stand and look at his father. "And you are?" I ask him.

"Name's Jackson," he says, extending his hand. We shake. The man is broad-shouldered and handsome, with gentle but sad eyes. Though I can tell we're around the same age, a hard life has taken its toll. He looks tired and worn down.

"You in charge here?" I ask.

"Not me, man. No thank you," he says. "But I can take you to who is."

Sweeping Jamal into his arms, Jackson leads me to the corner of the warehouse. There, a stairwell takes us to the basement. Down here, things get a lot darker and more ominous. Water drips from the concrete above, and bare bulbs cast harsh shadows on the walls. The soldiers from before, the ones who escorted me here, they're down here milling about, and they don't look so happy with me encroaching.

For the most part, the basement is an open expanse, save for the massive columns holding the weight of the floor above. But along the perimeter, using the same make-shift repurposed supplies, they've partitioned off various sections: a meeting room, a gym, an armory, and a firing range. But we keep walking until we reach a central control center.

A glass enclosure separates it from the rest of the basement. Stepping inside, I find the area to be temperature-controlled. Racks of servers, rows of computer terminals, and a wall of video screens hum with electricity. A handful of staff look up at me from their screens, but none seem surprised to see me.

"What is this place?" I ask, unnerved.

"A shelter. A school. A hospital," a woman says behind me. I turn and spot her approaching us. In her mid-fifties, she's confident and friendly; her smile seems sincere. "It's whatever we need it to be," she continues, extending her hand.

But I don't take it.

"More like a hide-out," I say. "You're radical extremists, aren't you? Anarchists?"

"I bet you'll call us godless next," a man says, stepping out from between computer servers. "Atheists, perhaps? Or whatever the network finds more triggering with its audience these days."

The man joins the woman, arms crossed, and I eye them both. Their age, their appearance: I remember learning about people like them. It was old timers like this that used to criticize the network. They'd cry about civil liberties and tyranny. They'd throw words around like 'state propaganda' and 'due process' — as if anybody cared about those things anymore. Then they turned to protests, then riots. I thought we stomped scum like this out for good.

"You're what's left of the old freedom movement, aren't you? You're terrorists," I say.

The woman laughs. "Mister Evans," she says. "Let me introduce us. This is my husband, Dean Destin. And I'm Janice." A married couple, I should've known. They even look alike, with faded freckles and streaks of grey. "I guess you can call us a movement," Janice continues. "We offer a better way of life than what's being forced on the people back where you come from."

I snort a laugh. This is predictable traditionalist drivel. They think *this*, living in a musty, dilapidated warehouse, is a better way of life. That *this* is somehow better than mass consumer consumption. I guess I shouldn't be surprised that they clumped together here in this shithole. Over the last century, the more severe the income inequality, the more people got pushed out of society altogether. After all, if you're not a consumer, what are you? But to see them so organized, that's shocking. These old Bills of Rights traditionalists still hold up the Constitution as if it still means something, as if it weren't simply a clever marketing device used to demand party loyalty.

But still, they shouldn't exist. *This* shouldn't exist.

"I've never seen anything like this," I say, gesturing about the building. "I've never even heard of anything like this."

"Of course not," Dean snickers. "Media coverage is everything, Mister Evans. You know that better than anybody. Without media coverage, one simply does not exist." He leans toward me, sure to have my attention. "If people don't know about us, they can't join us."

"Why did you bring me down here?" I ask, cutting to the chase. "What do you want?"

Janice steps forward. "To offer you an opportunity: the chance to join us. And do something right, something good."

"And that is?" I ask.

Janice and Dean exchange an uneasy glance — this conversation must not be going as they planned.

"Let me guess: a revolution?" I ask. Off their silence, I laugh. "So that's it, isn't it? This is transactional. You brought me down here, so I'd help you bring down *the network*, overthrow *the regime*," I say sarcastically, using air quotes. "And what do I get out of it?"

They look at each other, stumped.

"A community," Janice says. "Family."

I shake my head. People always want something from me: my money, my fame, my finger pulling a trigger. But since I turned on *The Eagle's Hammer*, I'm dead set on making my own decisions now.

Dean clears his throat as if he's about to make an important announcement. "It's true dualism, isn't it?" he asks condescendingly. "Taylor Evans, the mass-murdering monster. And Taylor Evans, our only hope and savior."

Dean shakes his head, snickering. But then, like flipping a switch, he's suddenly serious, glaring at me with pure hatred. "Make no mistake, Evans," he snaps. "You're no hero. Just because you had a change of heart, just because you let one target live, that doesn't make you a hero now. You're still a monster. A sick, soulless monster. You deserve to burn in hell, and I pray you will."

I blink. The man is right, and I agree with him. But this attitude from him, it's too much for me. Nobody raises their voice to me... not to Taylor Evans.

"I don't need this," I say defensively, turning toward the door. Janice leaps in front of me, blocking my way.

"Please. My husband," she says, lowering her voice to a gentle whisper. "He's lost a lot to the nats. And to the hammer…"

She trails off, then collects her thoughts. A new approach, perhaps? Her eyes meet mine. "You've lost a lot too, you know," she says, placing a hand on my chest. "They kidnapped you as a kid. They wiped your memory and inserted you into a cult of murder and death. And now, yeah, you made a choice. You decided not to kill. But the network is after you. Now, you're the target. And they won't stop — they can't stop — until you're dead."

She pauses, letting that all sink in… my victimhood. I look at her and consider what she's saying. It's true: they will hunt me down. But I'm not sure I can even process this at this point…

Emotions dull the blade.

Unsure of what to say, I find myself longing for the reassuring production chatter of my helmet's earpiece. Me, I wish somebody would just tell me my next line of dialogue…

"Just let him go," Dean says. "Let him walk away. He's a mindless automaton who doesn't know his left from his right if the network isn't telling him."

Losing my patience, I take a threatening step toward Dean, but Janice cuts me off. "I apologize," she says, directing me toward the exit. "You are our guest. And you are free to go. It's just that… we've been waiting for you."

I stop and cock my head.

"Waiting for me?" I ask.

Dean laughs — he's quite enjoying this. "We've been watching you, Evans," he says, gesturing toward the video screens.

On his cue, the video cuts to security camera footage. I recognize its location immediately: it's my building's lobby. And, from one corner of the screen to the other, I stroll on by… *What the hell?*

The footage cuts to another shot, this time a view of the foyer *inside* my condo. I exit the elevator and enter my home… *What in the actual fuck?*

I realize this is security footage from my penthouse, courtesy cameras I didn't know existed. Based on the time stamp, it's from the night before last. On-screen, I approach Candis passed out on the couch. I attempt to carry her to bed, but she lashes out. She falls out of my arms, landing hard on the floor.

The footage cuts again… to the master bathroom. I've stripped naked and am now staring at my reflection in the window, flexing like a narcissistic fool. I turn on the water and step into the shower…

The footage cuts again… and the image zooms in on my face; tears are streaking down my cheeks, my lips trembling. And I slowly slide down into the steam…

"What the hell is this?" I shout, enraged.

Janice backs away. Jamal slides behind his father's legs, hiding. Me, I can hardly breathe. Dean continues to laugh. He loves this. He loves this twist. On-screen, the sequence loops.

"We had a feeling you were having a change of heart," Dean says. "And here you are."

Me, I see nothing but red. I snap and lunge at Dean, grabbing him by the throat. The others in the room, the staff and technicians, they scramble for sidearms, unsure of what to do. But Dean just laughs in my face.

"What?" he asks. "You didn't know the network had you under constant surveillance? You, Taylor Evans, their golden boy? The network's biggest investment?" I stare at him, stunned. "Hey, man," Dean says, chuckling. "They kept tabs on you, so we kept tabs on you. Tapping into their camera system was easy pickings."

I release his collar and slowly back away. Every inch of me, every muscle, is contracted and tense. Janice approaches me and places a hand on my shoulder, but I pull away. The last thing I want is to feel the touch of another person, let alone her.

Instead, I head for the door. I want to get the fuck out of here. I want to head to California and face trial for my crimes. I want to face the punishment I'm due: death by execution…

"We knew the torment you were going through," Janice shouts, cutting through the storm in my head. "The pain and anguish. The torture you endured going through with their crimes night after night. And, please, believe me, we want to help."

This is transactional, I think. Now comes the pitch…

"Fight with us," she says. "With your training and leadership…" She looks around the room, her eyes meeting the gaze of the technicians and staff, of Jackson and Jamal. "We can keep them safe. We can protect them. With your help, we can inspire a new generation to join our cause… to fight for freedom."

"With your knowledge," Dean says, stepping up to his wife's side, "we can hack deeper into the network's mainframe. It'll make this security footage seem like a joke. We can pirate their signal, put them off-line."

I look at him — the thought of shutting down the network seems so impossible that it jars me. You might as well try to extinguish the sun, but Dean continues. "With you, Evans," he says, "we can bring this government to its knees."

I think of Hernandez and Milner. Now it's Janice and Dean. One set of puppet masters traded for another. I shake my head. These people are bat-shit crazy. I look around and size them up. Terrorists, that's what they are. People like them are why the hammer exists. Radical extremists. The slime of humanity.

"Your cause is not my cause," I say. "Go ahead and get yourselves killed. But your blood won't be on my hands. Not anymore."

Dean rolls his eyes — he's not going to beg me. Janice sighs in defeat. A heavy silence hangs in the air until it's shattered by a staff member sliding through the door, desperate and wide-eyed.

"It's Patrisse," he says, gasping for air. "Patrisse is their next target."

An image of Patrisse Flynn flashes in my mind. Their next target?

A collective gasp sweeps through the room. Jackson and Janice, they're stunned. Dean leaps toward a computer terminal.

"Get it on screen," he barks. "Now!" One by one, the image of me in my shower is replaced by the network's feed.

"Oh no," Janice says, raising a hand to her mouth. "Not Patrisse."

On-screen is Patrisse's profile picture — the same one I had seen on my helmet's display. The program cuts to an irate pundit — though the volume is muted, the man's eyes say it all: he's furious. He's practically foaming at the mouth. Along the bottom of the screen, a chyron graphic scrolls by: *Lover or Fanatic: Why would she risk everything to save Taylor Evans?*

I blink, stunned by the presumption. Without thinking, I read the scrolling information aloud. "Wanted for aiding and abetting a known fugitive." I inch closer to the display. "Associate producer defies *The Eagle's Hammer*," I continue to read, "aids Taylor Evans in escape."

I stop reading and stand silent, processing this.

Patrisse Flynn… she saved me.

CHAPTER 12

"Weapons," I say, turning away from the network feed. "I need weapons." Janice and Dean glance at each other. The rest of the room stares at me, uncertain. I am the enemy in their midst — a living, breathing Eagle's Hammer. And I want my talons.

"Look," I say. "Did she save me or not? If so, give me weapons. Now."

"We don't know," Janice says. "We don't have regular contact with her. And definitely not since last night."

"The network thinks she did," Jackson says, holding Jamal tight in his arms.

"Turn it up," Dean says, gesturing toward the feed. "Let's hear what they're saying."

A staff member unmutes the volume, and we watch the broadcast transfixed. The pundit on-screen clings to his chair as if he's about to fly off in a rage.

"I don't (beep)ing care how she (beep)ing did it," the man says, foaming at the mouth. "I just want to see that (beep)ing (beep) take the bullet that was meant for Evans. She must die!"

Patrisse Flynn, I think. This woman, this stranger: she sacrificed herself for me. I think of my hammermobile last night outside the target's home. I think of how it unlocked for me when it shouldn't have — after access to my weapons and gear had been cut off. It was my only chance, my only hope for survival. And it unlocked.

Granted, that access could have been a fluke. Since no hammer had ever run before, it's easy to imagine something falling through the cracks. But my gut, it tells me this Patrisse Flynn was responsible.

"I'm going," I say, determined.

"Jackson," Janice says. "Take Mister Evans to the armory."

Jackson flashes me a smile. "Let's go, boss," he says.

"Hold it," Dean says, blocking our way. He glances between us, then Janice. "Let's think this through. The network never discloses the identity of a target before a broadcast. Why?"

I consider, but the answer is obvious. Doing so gives the target a hell of an advantage. They can run and hide. They can hunker down and fight. Or, more likely, it provides the target a chance to kill themselves and their family too. Murder suicides have only become more popular since the show went on the air.

Watching me think, Dean nods.

"So why now?" he asks.

Janice steps forward. "There's never been a target who was a member of the production's staff," she says. "It's not like they could keep it a secret from themselves. She'd have found out eventually."

She has a point, but Dean shakes his head. "It's a trap," he says, matter of fact. He nods toward me. "They think he'll come back for her."

"But Dean," Janice says, approaching her husband. "What about Patrisse?"

Dean's eyes sink to the floor. "She knew the risks when she came to us, when she took the assignment." The room becomes uncomfortably quiet. Jamal squirms in his father's arms. Dean glances at his staff. "We all know how dangerous this is. To risk everything we've built, everything we've accomplished… that'd be the last thing Patrisse would want. And you all know that. Now stop this rescue business. Nobody is going anywhere."

"I'm going," I say, stepping around him and marching toward the door. "With or without your help."

"Like a trained monkey," Dean snorts, waving me off. But the room stares at him in disgust. Even Janice doesn't hide her disappointment. Dean rolls his eyes. But then he caves.

"Wait," he shouts, catching me in the doorway. "Jackson," he says. "Give him anything he wants. Then take him as far as the Ben Franklin Bridge." He looks at me. "But let me make myself clear. I don't like this, Evans. But I don't like you either. If Patrisse dies, I'll know she died doing what was right. But as for you, if you get yourself killed…" He trails off, then smiles. "I might just grab a bag of fresh popcorn and enjoy the show."

Not waiting for Jackson to lead, I turn and beeline out the door. We cross toward the makeshift armory, and I find a teenager stationed at the counter, a twelve-gauge shotgun on his lap. He's one of the soldiers that escorted me here. But seeing him in the light, he doesn't look nearly as seasoned as he did before.

Watching me enter, the teen is unsure of how to present himself. When Jackson follows me in — Jamal still cradled in his arms — he breathes a sigh of relief.

"You see this shit, Jackson?" the kid asks, pointing at a television. "They're going after Patrisse."

Jackson nods. Stepping up to the counter, he sets Jamal on top and leans next to him. The three of them watch me walk up and down the aisle of wire shelves. This armory is a joke. The selection is so sparse and random, you'd think we were at a consignment shop. The weapons, they're laughable. A dull knife. A rusty revolver. A mid-century hunting rifle.

I glare back at the guys. "Is this all you got?" I ask, thinking of the armed soldiers in the sewers. I glance at the shotgun in the teen's hands: it looks like the good stuff's been claimed. Jackson shrugs. He reaches down toward a basket, then tosses me a brick of C-4.

Catching it, I can't help but laugh.

"It's demolition grade," Jackson says. "Still good." He tosses me another, and I catch that brick too.

"You really are a bunch of terrorists," I say, half-joking. In my hand, this is enough C-4 to bring down a bridge. I raise the dirty-white slab to my nose, noting the explosive's distinct smell — like motor oil. "You want me to blow her up, don't you?"

"Or yourself," Jackson says, smirking.

"Got any blasting caps?" I ask.

"Aisle two, sir," he says. "And thanks for shopping with us today."

I grab a moldy gym bag off a shelf and stuff the explosives inside. Slinging the bag over my shoulder, I continue on. Most of this junk looks to be old police issues, either tossed away or stolen when police departments were disbanded in favor of the nats. These rifles and pistols probably should have been melted down long ago. But when there's such a ridiculous overabundance of something, it's easy to lose track. Imagine outlawing screwdrivers, and you get the idea.

An ammo box catches my eye — it looks military, and I peer inside. A few dozen Army-issue grenades lay piled atop of each other. I pick one up and feel its weight.

"What about these?" I ask.

"Not a bad egg in the batch," Jackson shouts.

I stuff a few in my duffle and move along. I find a sad-looking, desert-used Beretta M9. The handgun pales compared to my trusted Colt/Detonics hybrid — the one I blew up in the microwave — but it's a solid option. I grab the weapon and the box of rounds beneath it.

Sure, these weapons aren't ideal. But I don't plan on defending the Alamo. And staying light on my feet has a more tactical advantage than rolling up in a Howitzer. All I want to do is save the girl's life... then I'm done. Distraction will be key. As my escape last night proved, anything off-script derails the production. So, my best bet is to be unpredictable.

With that in mind, I scan the armory one last time. In the corner, I spot a redheaded fireman ax. Picking it up, I flash a smile… I'm starting to enjoy this. *Be unpredictable.*

I slide the ax into my bag, letting the wood handle stick out the opening. Joining back up with Jackson and Jamal, the teenager looks me over.

"You gonna save Patrisse?" he asks, nervous.

"Yeah," I say.

The kid nods, then hands me the shotgun. "Take this," he says. Jackson raises an eyebrow — it's a generous offer. I take the weapon and inspect it. The barrel seems straight, and the action is adequately oiled.

"Thanks," I say.

Jackson lifts Jamal into his arms. "Now, let's get you a change of clothes," he says, looking me over head to toe. "Can't have you running around looking like a lost hammer."

He leads me back upstairs to his private room. Separated by tarps, it's the size of a closet. Children's toys are strewn about the tiny cot, and several old, water-stained photos are tacked up near the pillow.

While Jackson rummages through his things, gathering items for me, I lean down and take a closer look at the photographs. In them, a young woman blows out a birthday cake. In another, she graduates high school. In another, she's painting the walls of a home. I glance between her image and Jamal. There's a definite resemblance.

"His mother?" I ask.

Jackson realizes I'm fixed on the photographs. He hardens. "Yeah," he says, handing me an outfit. He turns to his boy and tugs on his sleeve. "Let's let the man get changed."

They turn toward the door. Reading Jackson, I can tell the mere inquiry stung him. "Where is she?" I ask, catching him.

Jackson hesitates and glares at the floor. "She's not here," he says, then exits.

She's dead, I think. They had a life together, a child. Undressing, I pause to consider whether she died at the hands of the hammer. My mouth goes dry as it dawns on me that I may have pulled the trigger.

I glance at the photos again, my eyes darting from one to the other, studying her features. But there have been so many targets — so many victims — I can't recall them all. I button my shirt, then slide on the canvas jacket when Janice pokes her head in.

"May I come in?" she asks.

"Yeah," I say. Janice pushes through the flap and enters. She stands awkwardly before me, nervous. "What is it?" I ask.

"You probably don't think you belong here with us," she says. I force a laugh. Sitting down on the cot, I gesture toward the photographs behind me.

"Lady, I probably killed this guy's wife," I say. Reaching into the duffle bag for the Beretta, I feel Janice tense up — her silence seems like all the confirmation I need. "I don't belong anywhere," I say, releasing the gun's magazine. Placing the box of ammo next to me, I begin loading rounds. "I'm a monster. Killing people is what I do."

Janice sits, then studies me. "The Latin etymology of monster is *monstrum*," she says. "Defined as a person or thing that is strange and out of place, but not necessarily evil. You," she says, taking my hand. "You are strange and out of place here with us, yes. But that doesn't mean you're evil."

I stand up and turn my back toward her. "I'll tell you what this boils down to," I say, slapping the magazine back in place. "Living and breathing. Dead or alive. It's binary, lady. Like a light switch. And me, I flip that switch down. These people," I say, motioning outside the room, "they won't forget that. And they shouldn't forget that."

Janice nods. "If you save her," she says, staring at the floor. "They'll come for you."

"The hammer?" I ask, sliding on the jacket.

"The hammer. The network. The nats. Yeah," she says, nodding. "Any chance of them letting you run off, to disappear and never be seen or heard of again, will be gone. They'll come for you, wherever you are. And they won't stop until you're dead."

I nod — that sounds right up my alley. I stuff the handgun behind my waist and sling the duffle bag over my shoulder — all set and ready.

"What's her address?" I ask.

CHAPTER 13

Slipping through an exhaust vent, we exit the sewer and emerge at the riverbank. The Ben Franklin Bridge is on our right, a massive steel suspension bridge that spans the river. Every day, thousands of pedestrians walk to and from the city of Philadelphia on the other side. Most are day laborers hoping to make enough money to feed their families, their desperation permanently smeared on their faces.

Eyeing the stairs up to the walkway, I notice Jackson and Jamal approach a chain link fence that overlooks the water. On the river, tugboats push sludge barges downstream.

"He likes to watch the boats," Jackson says to me over his shoulder.

Stepping next to the father and son, I feel the cold breeze on my face. I close my eyes and think of the kid's mother. My thoughts slide to the nameless horde who haunts me, the hundreds of targets I've executed, their eyes glossed over, their expressions blank...

Victims. I should call them what they are. They're victims. They're victims of me, yeah. I pulled the trigger. I blew their brains out. But they're also victims of this society. They're victims of a million decisions that lead to this reality. Seemingly innocent decisions at the time, sure. But compiled, it's those decisions that led to this nightmare. It's those decisions that killed these victims. And yeah, the kid's mother is one of them.

I open my eyes and find Jamal watching me like a hawk. This kid, when in his father's arms, is fearless.

"Are you a good guy or a bad guy?" he asks.

Me, I struggle to answer.

"Well?" he asks, pulling two action figures out of his fanny pack. I look at Jackson — he shrugs back at me, then laughs.

A good guy or a bad guy? Until yesterday, I thought I was a good guy. I was doing what society wanted of me. But now, just hours on the run, I don't know anymore. I look across the water at the city, and there it is waiting for me: Trucast Tower. The root of all evil.

Always know your way home, Milner said to me — that was yesterday morning. Had you asked me then, I'd have told you that anybody caught gallivanting with domestic terrorists was a terrorist themselves — punishable by death. And I would've been happy to deliver that punishment. But now...

A bad guy? Or good?

This kid has stumped me. I feel him watching me, analyzing me with a child's innocence. I look at him, into his little brown eyes.

"What do you think?" I ask.

Jamal looks at the two action figures in his hands. One of them is a good guy, the other bad. He looks from the toys to me, then back.

"I think," he says, deciding, "you're good." Jamal offers me the toy. "Here you go."

I blink, stunned by his generosity. I take the action figure into my hand. It seems so tiny in my palm.

"Thanks," I say.

"Don't lose him," Jamal says, stern.

"No, sir," I say, pocketing the toy.

"Can you find your way from here?" Jackson asks.

"Yeah," I nod, gazing up toward the bridge. "You think she'll be there?"

"She'll be there," he says. "She's not one to back down from a fight." Jackson reaches into his pocket and pulls out a phone terminal. "Here," he says, handing it to me. "Use it to keep tabs on tonight's broadcast. But chuck it after that, or they'll zero in on its signal."

I inspect the phone. Both the front and backside cameras have been removed. Assuming the microphone is deactivated, this should prevent any facial or voice recognition programs from identifying me as well.

"Thank you, man," Jackson says, extending his hand. Looking me in the eye, we shake. It's a gentle but firm squeeze that has me thinking I might not have killed the kid's mother after all. "Good luck," Jackson says.

"Good luck," the boy parrots.

Waving my goodbye, I climb the stairs and join the flow of pedestrians crossing the bridge. Most of them carry the tools of their trade, so even my duffle bag isn't out of place. Covering myself with my tattered blanket, I blend right in with the crowd.

As I walk, I wonder how Candis is taking the news of my desertion. I can imagine her overwhelming confusion, still high on whatever drugs she took during last night's broadcast. Did it even register to her? I can picture her passed out on the sofa as, on-screen, I evaded Blair. I can see her eyes flutter open, struggling to focus on the television as my car crashed into the river. It probably wasn't until this morning that she fully processed what I had done.

If she thought me a monster before, what does she think of me now?

It wasn't always terrible between us. We had good times — at least, I think we did. Photos of our extravagant, decadent lifestyle littered our social media accounts. Date night would include a private jet to Acadia National Park, all at the expense of whatever natural gas corporation was vying for drilling rights. The selfies she'd post would include us on romantic getaways; she'd hang around my neck, pouting her lips and winking at the camera. The posts would garner hundreds of thousands of likes and shares, sometimes millions. But I can't remember a single conversation between us.

Now, here I am. A moldy blanket wrapped around me, walking with the silent underclass. I feel like an alien amongst them, a creature from another world. Have I faced hardships? Have I struggled? Not like these people. I am a prince among them. Well-fed and well-groomed. My teeth are white, and my posture is perfect. And yet, these are the people the hammer hits hardest.

Hernandez would say these people deserve the punishment. She'd say these people are perfectly capable of pulling themselves up and out of poverty if they were so inclined.

But is that true? I didn't choose to be a hammer. I simply was. These people? They didn't choose to be poor.

The bridge is a few thousand feet long. From the walkway, I watch the autonomous tractor-trailers hauling cargo into and out of the city. Every few minutes, a subway train races below, screeching on its tracks. Other than that, the march is solemn and quiet, and my thoughts linger on the one question I can't quite answer: why?

Why am I here? Why am I doing this? Why am I putting my life on the line for some woman I don't even know, who I don't give a shit about?

Jackson's kid would say I'm doing this because I'm a good guy — but I've never done anything good in my life. No, I think, shaking away any righteousness I may be feeling, I'm doing this for one reason: answers.

I want to know why she did it, why she saved me. Just like I have no reason to save her, she had no reason to save me. In this world, heroics don't get you shit, except a target on your back. But the only thing keeping me from just walking away, from hopping on a train and disappearing, is this one nagging question: why?

Maybe Janice and Dean — and this laughable resistance they head — are behind it. Patrisse was their plant, after all, their mole on the inside. But Janice and Dean seemed legitimately jarred when they discovered that Patrisse was the next target. So maybe Patrisse acted alone, a rogue agent who decided to shake things up, big time. But this logic just circles my thoughts back to the original question: why?

I get an answer to that. Then I'm gone.

Feeling the breeze on my face again, I imagine walking all the way to California. I imagine the UCC authorities taking me in and placing me under arrest. I imagine them charging me with crimes against humanity. And, since I'm daydreaming here, I imagine Milner and Hernandez in the courtroom with me as the judge reads our verdicts.

Guilty. Guilty. Guilty.

Our punishment: death by lethal injection. And I take pleasure in knowing that Milner and Hernandez will answer for their sins. That they'll die right alongside me...

The walkway dumps us out at Franklin Square, and the pedestrians scatter in all directions. Me, I turn right and head north. From here, it's only a few miles to Kensington, the neighborhood where Patrisse lives. And that's good: it's already early evening. The sun will set soon, and the cover of darkness only plays to my advantage.

Walking through the city, I thread along side streets and back alleys where I'm less likely to run into a nat patrol. This neighborhood is littered with century-old, dilapidated tenements. But it's also full of abandoned construction sites. Trash collects in the unfinished condominiums, reminders of the aborted economic progress of the last fifty years and the slow death of the nation's middle class.

I turn a corner and find myself on her block. The street is quiet, but I pull the blanket tight. Her apartment building looks like every other structure in the neighborhood. If it weren't for the dim lights in the windows, you'd think it was condemned.

My phone buzzes. It's the national Eagle's Hammer notification. Looking up through people's curtains, I see their televisions automatically flick to the network's coverage. It's not a stretch to think that most viewers have been waiting for this moment.

Well, it's showtime, folks. Get ready.

Out of morbid curiosity, I pull the phone out of my pocket. I've never seen *The Eagle's Hammer* on this end; as a viewer. The lights fade up in the studio, revealing Silas and Skylar seated at their anchor desk. They look so fake, I think, watching them live for the first time.

"Crime is out of control," Skylar says, on the verge of hysterics. Blah, blah, blah.

I've seen enough. And I'm out of time.

I cross the street, beelining for the building's entrance. Stepping inside, I find two men milling in the foyer, each watching the program on their phone. Though dressed in civilian clothing, undercover nats are easy to spot. I'm surprised by their presence, however — why are they here? This is highly unorthodox — the network and the nats seldom work together — but what do I care? They're in my way; that's all that matters.

"Buildings closed," one of them says, barely looking away from his phone. "Get your ass outta here."

The other guy, I feel him size me up. There's a moment where our eyes meet. And in that instant, we both know what will happen next.

This is not a drill...

The guy reaches for his gun. But before he can warn his colleague, before he can utter a single word, I make my move…

Trust me; it happens fast. Real fast.

Dropping the duffel bag, I toss the blanket over his head. His colleague, he finally looks up. But as he draws his weapon, I kick him square in the throat, feeling his trachea collapse through the sole of my boot.

That guy, he stumbles into the wall, gasping for air. Unable to make a sound, he watches in horror as I grab hold of the blanket, twist it around his buddy's head, then swing him face-first into the wall. The guy falls to the floor limp, blood soaking through the blanket's fabric.

Knowing he's next, the other guy tries to scream — but all he can manage is a painful gurgle. I shake my head — what a pathetic piece of shit.

Warmed up now, I'm feeling loose and having fun. There may not be any cameras here, there may not be anybody watching at home, but for this kill, I go big. I go for spectacle.

Winding up, I deliver a brutal roundhouse kick. His head snaps back, and he crumbles. The poor guy might still have a pulse down there on the floor — but his thinking days are done.

Now, both of their phones lay on the tile, the broadcast still on their screens. And I can't help but glance down and check where the show is. "Because *The Eagle's Hammer*," Skylar says, still reading from the teleprompter.

"Is about to drop," Silas says, joining her.

But instead of cutting to the dazzling, graphics-heavy show open, the program cuts to a live shot of Trucast Tower — *this is different.* The music is rocking as the team's hammermobiles race out of the building. They're not even bothering to launch from the Eagle's Nest — *another first.* I pause and listen to the silent street outside the doorway — the calm before the storm.

They'll be here any minute now.

I charge up the stairs and reach Patrisse's apartment. I knock at her door. No answer. But just as I'm about to knock again, the door swings open, and it's Patrisse Flynn, her Trucast employee badge still hanging from a lanyard around her neck. She looks me over without the slightest hint of surprise on her face.

"I don't have time for this," she says. As she swings the door shut, I jam my foot inside.

"I'm here to save you," I say.

"I know," Patrisse says, shoving me. "And I don't have time for that." Over her shoulder, I glimpse a pile of hard drives and computer terminals on the floor.

"Listen," I say, pulling the ax from my bag. Patrisse backs away, unsure of my intentions. "I am here," I say, nice and slow, and with gravitas, "to save you."

CHAPTER 14

You, you're sitting at home as the hammermobiles roar through Kensington. You, your husband, and that kid of yours, you all watch as they race up to Patrisse's building. The three of you — and just about every soul in America — watch as Samra takes the lead. But the whole mood tonight is different, almost cheerful.

Gone is the dread.

Gone is the terror.

For the first time in the show's history, everybody watching knows one thing for sure: they're not the target — unless you're Patrisse Flynn, that is.

Samra steps onto the curb, the cameras buzzing around him. He looks up at the building and waits for the rest of the team to hit their marks. Then he says it: his very own catchphrase already trademarked and licensed for the masses: "Let's hammer this."

But it's not the same. And everything about it — his voice, his delivery — it's wrong. You and your husband, you can't help but snicker.

But your kid cringes. This morning you watched as he tossed his official Taylor Evans action figure into the back of the closet. He even covered the toy with a blanket as if the action figure's cold, painted-on, and traitorous eyeballs were too much to bear...

The hammers maneuver into the building and find the two bodies in the lobby, lying in pools of blood. You, you see them on your television and gasp. But the commentators back in the studio, they're too busy graveling on about how thrilling and historic it all is even to notice.

But the hammers do.

They stare at the bodies uneasily until Riley shouts in their ears to keep moving. Samra darts up the stairs first, and the others follow. Reaching the apartment door, he falls back to let Riggs take her position — she's been tasked with busting open the door. Menial work at best. She places her shotgun on the doorknob, then waits for the cue. Samra's eyes narrow, then he nods.

BOOM.

Riggs blows a hole in the door where the lock had been, then spins and kicks it open. Samra steps quickly into the dark, smoke-filled apartment, his gun drawn. But Patrisse and I, we're nowhere to be found. Instead, that pile of hard drives, mobile devices, IDs, and credit cards, it's all just burning right there in front of them. The smoke is thick and toxic, and it pours out into the hall.

As for the windows, they're covered by her mattress and the living room couch, its cushions stuffed in the cracks. No light's getting in, not even from the hover-units outside the building.

"What the hell is this?" Riggs asks, peering over Samra's shoulder — they've never seen anything like this.

Annoyed by Riggs's outburst, Samra inches forward. His eyes dart about the living room before settling on the wall-mounted video screen. Finding himself on the broadcast, he pauses to admire his profile until he hears the faint sound of a pin tapping. He turns toward the door frame, and, yep, now he sees it...

A pin hangs from the door via a string. But not just any pin... a grenade pin. Samra spins to find the grenade I duct-taped to the wall, now pinless and armed.

His eyes go wide... KA-BOOM.

The blast engulfs Samra, sending him back into the hall. He slams into the banister, rolls over it, then falls to the lobby below. He lands with a thud and burns motion-less. The rest of the team stares at him, stunned.

"Fuck this," Riggs says. She swings her gun toward the door. The hover-cams barely have time to clear out before she opens fire. The rest of the team follows suit. Together, they blast the apartment with hundreds of rounds, shred-ding the interior. The onslaught cuts through the mattress and couch, shattering the windows and raining glass on the street below.

Finally, the team lets off, their barrels smoking. Riggs cautiously pokes her head inside, then pulls back. "Can't see shit in there," she says.

A pair of cameras swoop over her and enter. "Looks clear," Riley says in their ears. Riggs and CJ exchange an uneasy glance, shaking their heads with frustration.

"Fubar already," CJ says under his breath. But he takes the lead, his boots crunching on the crumbled plaster as he enters. Riggs and the others follow along, cautiously moving from one room to the next.

Kitchen: clear. Bathroom: clear. Bedroom: clear. Room by room, they approach the last of the bedrooms, its door shut. But between Riggs, CJ, and Gorman, neither of them wants to be the one to open it — not after what happened to Samra.

"Keep moving," Riley says.

CJ and Riggs look at Gorman.

"You're up, buttercup," Riggs says to him.

Gorman sighs. He squares up to the door, takes a deep breath, and kicks. CJ and Riggs peer into the room and find that a gaping hole has been chopped into the wall clear through to the apartment next door. This was my doing.

The hammers stare dumbfounded into the darkness but see nothing. "Bet this shit's booby-trapped," Riggs says, unnerved.

"Enough talking," Riley says. "CJ, it's your kill. Now go."

Riggs flashes him a smile. "It's all you, amigo," she says, sarcastic. "America's watching."

CJ shakes his head but does as ordered. He carefully extends one foot through the opening and places it on the carpeted floor… so far, so good. He shifts his weight entirely into the other apartment, then pulls his leg through.

"Clear," CJ says, waving his comrades over.

Riggs and Gorman cautiously follow. With the three of them fixated on what lies ahead, none of them notice me sneaking back into the apartment through the battered front door, the ax held high above my head.

Even the hover-cameras are oblivious as I inch up behind them. Then, I chop the nearest one to the floor. It sparks and sputters, then dies.

"Woah," Riley says, loud enough that I can hear him through the team's earpieces. "What the hell happened to camera two?"

Gorman, bringing up the rear, is halfway through the hole when he looks back and spots me. "Evans! It's Evans," he shouts, fumbling with his machine gun. As he swings it my way, I chop it right out of his hands — this ax is fun.

The gun clangs to the floor.

"Get out of the way, Gorman," CJ says, peering around him, trying to spot me.

"Evans is back in the target's flat," Riggs relays to the production staff.

"Take him out," Riley screams. "Take him out!"

CJ and Riggs grab Gorman and yank him back through the hole. When they finally clear him, they turn around and find me jeering at them. Riggs bulls her way into the opening, eager for the kill. "He's mine!" she shouts.

She opens fire, decimating another of the hover-cams. The drone explodes in a spectacular shower of sparks. The flash is bright enough that Riggs can't help but look away, shielding herself...

That's when I lob another grenade at them. For them, I understand their confusion. Out of the void comes the explosive, and it bounces right between the three of them.

Staring at it on the floor, Riggs shakes her head. "That little shit…"

KA-BOOM.

The blast throws the three of them against the walls as the shrapnel knocks the last hover-cam out of service — blinding the production staff. Riggs, CJ, and Gorman collapse in agony. Lucky for them, their armor absorbed most of the damage — but they'll be feeling this for weeks.

You, you watch the camera feed flicker and die. The network is momentarily in black before abruptly cutting to the studio. Silas and Skylar are caught by surprise. But with no more cameras in the apartment, Riley has nowhere else to go. A moment passes, then fake smiles splash onto their faces.

"It appears," Silas stammers, staring at his tally light, "we're experiencing technical difficulties…"

Me, I'm charging up the stairs with Patrisse. We reach the roof access, and with one swing of the ax, I snap the lock. Hurrying outside, a cold wind greets us.

Patrisse looks at me critically. "Now what?"

I drop the bag, and Patrisse peers over my shoulder as I reach inside for the shotgun. I stand up, rack the slide, then wait. My eyes search the sky above us as I listen. Patrisse grows impatient. She wants to run, and I don't blame her.

Then we hear it: the buzz of approaching hover-cams. They know we're up there, but that's no surprise. There are probably a half dozen high-altitude reconnaissance drones mapping the area. But these hover-cams — if I can take them out, we've got a chance.

I line one up in my sights and pull the trigger. BAM. The camera explodes. As the shot rings out, I rack another round. The hover-cams scatter, but I still have clear shots on them. BAM. Another one drops out of the sky. BAM. Then another. BAM. And another...

Out of ammo, I toss the gun and turn to Patrisse.

"Now we run," I say.

This neighborhood is full of row houses and tenements, their roofs right next to each other, clear to the elevated subway track. And that's our escape. The remaining hover-cams will chase us; that's what they do. But if we make it to cover, then we're in the clear.

But Patrisse, she's foraging through the duffle bag. She finds the explosive and laughs. "Jackson give you this?" she asks, showing me.

I shrug, then nod. Now I'm the impatient one.

"Let's go," I say, my teeth clenched. I grab her wrist and pull her toward the ledge. She doesn't hold back, not for

long. In one swift movement, we leap from one rooftop...
to another.

"Keep moving," I say, glancing back at the next salvo of
drones on their way. But Patrisse, she's next to me, stride for
stride. We jump... and land on another building.

We leap... and land on another.

I reach into the duffle bag, pulling out the handgun.
Hopefully, this damn antique doesn't explode in my hand.
We jump again, the hover-cams now buzzing around us
like angry hornets. Landing hard, I roll into a crouching
position, gun at the ready.

BAM. BAM. BAM.

I pick off a few more hover-cams. They putter, then
crash to the street below.

"Let's go," I say. And we run and jump again. But
landing, we find the next lot is empty — which certainly
fucks up my plan.

Dammit, I know this neighborhood. I've studied it.
Nowhere was it documented that the next building had
been leveled or that it was even slated for demolition.
Patrisse and I, we step up to the ledge — it's three stories
down, no fire escape, not even a trash-filled dumpster to
drop into.

"Shit," Patrisse says.

I turn back, looking around for access into the building. But there's nothing. The structure is clearly condemned. A large hole sags into the collapsing roof, revealing water-logged beams inside.

Across the street, catty-corner to where we're at, are the elevated tracks of the Market-Frankford Line, one of the city's two subway systems. If that damn building was still there, I had hoped to climb down a fire escape and make a run for Tioga station. But now...

Now we're fucked.

"What did I tell you about finding your way home, Evans?" a voice calls out, startling us. We turn to find Milner suddenly up here as if appearing out of thin air; a submachine gun aimed our way. He chuckles at our confusion. Milner — the son of a bitch is cunning. He knew exactly what I'd do and where I'd go...

But of course he did; he trained me. He thinks like me because he taught me to think. And looking at him now, decked out in revamped Eagle's Hammer armor and gear, how fucking predictable this is too.

"Out of retirement?" I ask. "That didn't take long. Network must be desperate."

"Blood's addictive, boy. You never do lose a taste for it, believe me," he says, inching toward us.

"Now drop the gun and bag. Get your hands above your head."

Patrisse and I comply. I toss the gun toward Milner and let the strap slide off my shoulder. The bag thuds on the tar paper.

"I'll be honest with you, Evans," Milner says. "If Hernandez wanted you dead, you'd be dead already."

I cock my head, perplexed. "Hammers don't take prisoners," I say.

Milner smirks, then nods. "Look around, Evans," he says, gesturing. "No cameras. No other hammers. This isn't a part of the show. This is real, son. Hand over the girl and come with me. The network has plans for you. You'll see. Hernandez, she'll have this all worked out. Trust me. She's invested a lot in you, and it'd be a shame to spill it all here."

Bullshit, I think. Why would Hernandez want me alive? She wouldn't, not after last night. If anything, a public hanging is more likely. But Milner has a point: the sky is silent. No drones, no cameras. And this, capturing the fugitive Taylor Evans: this is must-see TV.

"Let's go, Evans," Milner says.

"And what if I don't?" I ask. "You'll kill me?"

Milner snorts, then shrugs. "Killing you —
America's golden boy — that's one order I'd be all too
happy to execute," he says. "But that's not my order,
not today."

"Fuck this," Patrisse says, suddenly dropping to
her knees. Milner and I both watch, stunned, as she
reaches into the bag.

"Get up," Milner shouts, furious. "Now!"

"The thing about Jackson," Patrisse says, ignoring
Milner and glancing up at me. "He knows what a
girl needs."

Milner fires a warning shot into the air. But
Patrisse, she's fearless. Ignoring him, she quickly
jams the blasting cap into the brick of C-4, effectively arming the explosive — this girl knows what
she's doing.

She stands back up, hands raised. Milner is clueless
as to what she's done. But, glaring at her, he spits in
her direction. "Listen, girl," Milner says. "When I tell
you to do something…"

Patrisse and I, our eyes meet. I thought she
was afraid — but she projects anything but. Then
she winks at me and kicks the bag through the
collapsed roof…

I watch wide-eyed as the bag and explosives disappear into the building. The three of us standing there on the rooftop, we listen to the bag hit this and that as it seemingly falls deep into the structure. And then... BOOM.

An explosion rattles the entire building. Milner and I lock eyes. He shakes his head ever so slightly, but a smile creeps onto his face. He both hates what she's done and loves what she's done. Patrisse, she backs away. At this point, Milner has more important things to worry about than Patrisse Flynn, and he knows it...

Another explosion rings out from the structure's depths. Then another, more violent and destructive — a gas line, perhaps? Deep inside, columns crumble, beams splinter, and floors buckle. The entire foundation shudders.

Once it begins, there's going to be no stopping it...

The entire rooftop drops a few feet, maybe more, as the building begins to pancake. The three of us, we stand there, arms outstretched, keeping our balance, as the structure starts to list.

Oh, yeah — this building is going down...

CHAPTER 15

Three hundred and fifty tons. That's how much a building like this weighs. Three hundred and fifty tons of concrete and brick, plaster and plumbing, radiators and abandoned furniture. And right now, all three stories of it are tipping over like a tree falling in a forest.

With the roof sagging beneath our feet, Patrisse grabs my wrist. She pulls away from the direction the building is listing. As the pitch increases, we scurry over the ledge, splaying ourselves out on the side of the building. The structure buckles, then rips itself apart as it topples.

The brunt of the building slams into the elevated subway track across the street, snapping guide wires and smashing light posts as it dumps Patrisse and me on the platform.

The rest of it collapses into the street itself. Debris rains down, and a thick, asbestos-laden cloud envelopes the block but Patrisse and I are atop the rubble — and alive.

Coughing and spitting, I scan the wreckage. I've got to find Milner. But I don't see him, not up here, at least. I approach the railing, or what's left of it, and peer down at the street below. Through the dust, I spot him. He's alive and climbing to his feet. He looks up at me, then grins.

Me, I'm not sure whether I'm relieved or disappointed that he survived.

"Well," Patrisse says, still huffing. "That was a hell of a ride."

"Blowing up a building?" I ask, agitated by her quip. "You don't know who was in there. You don't know who might have been beneath us," I say, pointing at the destruction along the street.

Listen to me: I sound like I care.

Patrisse glares at me. "Oh, fuck off," she says.

The subway track beneath us begins to rumble. At first, I think the whole platform is compromised, that the structure itself will soon collapse. But then the emergency brakes of an approaching subway train screech. The train and its headlight emerge from the dust, stopping just before the debris.

I charge up to the conductor's enclosed cab and rap on the window. Both star-struck and terrified, the conductor opens the door, and we step inside. "Now reverse the train," I say. "Back the way you came."

The conductor nods. Without taking his eyes off me, he flips a large switch to reverse, then slowly pushes the throttle lever up — the train heads down the track toward the city.

Me, I close my eyes and clear my head. The further away from Milner we get, the better. But what then, I have no idea. I open my eyes and find Patrisse watching me. I expect her to turn away as I stare back at her — to wilt and submit. But she does not.

The conductor's phone sits atop the control panel, still broadcasting the network's coverage. The chatter draws my attention to the screen, and I see the flicker of footage being replayed: our big escape. I nudge the conductor and nod toward his phone.

"How was the show tonight?" I ask condescendingly.

"Good," he says, uncertain.

"Oh yeah?" I ask. "What was your favorite part?"

He looks uneasily between Patrisse and me. "When you blew up the old folk's home," he says.

"What?" Snatching his phone, Patrisse and I watch the feed. Recorded from a distance, footage of the building toppling plays in slow-motion. The chyron along the bottoms reads: *Terrorist attack levels nursing home. Taylor Evans responsible.*

"Nursing home?" I ask.

Patrisse just laughs. Me, I look at the conductor. Then I glance out the window into the passenger compartment of the train. A dozen riders stare back at me, each holding their own phones in hand, some recording me with their cameras.

"For fuck's sake," I say. Frustrated, I pull the conductor out of his seat and push him through the door into the other compartment. "Go. Get going. Get the fuck out of here. And take your damn phone with you," I add, tossing the device at him.

Stopping there in the doorway, I look at the stunned passengers. "It wasn't a nursing home," I shout before slamming the door shut.

"The network's wasting no time spinning this one," Patrisse says, smirking.

"Yeah, well. It's bullshit," I say.

Patrisse looks me over, sizing me up. And I realize this is the first time I've been alone with this woman, the first time

I've been in her presence. We sit in silence as the train races along the tracks, blowing by stations.

"Now what?" she asks.

"Now nothing," I quip. "Next stop, I jump off, and I'm gone. You, you'll never see me again. Nobody will ever see me again."

She nods but says nothing.

Me, I reach into my jacket pocket and pull out the action figure Jamal had given me earlier, along the river. I turn it over in my hand, then give it to Patrisse.

"This Jamal's?" she asks.

"Give it back to him for me," I say.

"Is that it?" Patrisse asks, studying the toy. "You're just going to walk away?"

"You saved me," I say. "I saved you. Makes us even."

Patrisse snorts, then laughs. "I didn't save you," she says, shaking her head. "I wouldn't risk my neck for you, not in a million years." I glance at her but then look away. "I worked way too long, far too hard to risk it all on you," she adds.

I blink. I think of my hammermobile. I think of it unlocking when it shouldn't have, providing my get-away. "Then how…" I begin to ask, but she cuts me off.

"Gross incompetence is my guess," Patrisse says. "That's standard operating procedure for the network. For this country, isn't it? Hell, if bullets didn't shoot straight, you'd all be fucked."

I stand awkwardly next to Patrisse. I wish I had a gun in my hand, not that I would kill her. But so I could check its magazine, chamber another round, prepare for whatever comes next. The motion, the sound of the action, would be comforting. But instead, I stand here swaying with the movement of the subway.

"Sorry to burst your bubble, stud," Patrisse continues, enjoying my discomfort. "Had it been me, I'd have let them kill you."

I nod. I attempt to say something… but I've got nothing. No witty comeback or biting retort. Nothing. I don't know which is worse: still not knowing who saved me and why — or feeling like a fool in front of Patrisse. None of my training prepared me for this.

Nearing Center City, the train passes beneath the Ben Franklin Bridge. As the tracks turn to head underground, the lights of the subway car flicker, then go out. The train begins to slow, the dead weight of the cars squealing on the tracks. Patrisse and I look at each other.

"Somebody's killed power to the line," I say.

The train comes to a stop. In the other compartment, the passengers peer out the windows, panicked and scared. A flashlight sweeps down the tunnel, then into a window.

"They're looking for us," I say, pulling Patrisse to the floor. I crawl over to the door and listen. Outside, boots crunch on the gravel. A hushed voice directs the group, sending them this way and that. They're going to check the cars, one by one.

Now I really wish I had a gun. I think of where I had thrown it on the rooftop. Who knows where it ended up in the rubble. I'm not afraid of hand-to-hand combat; in fact, I welcome the challenge, but who knows how many nats are out there, ready for war.

Peeking through the cracks of the door, I spot a guy posted outside. Weapon or not, I have to act. I give Patrisse a curt nod, then kick open the door. I catch the guy before he turns around, placing him in a neck hold. The guy submits instantly, letting his rifle swing to his side and raising his hands.

"Easy, Evans," the guy whimpers. "Take it easy." The other militants spin toward us, their flashlights catching me. I'm surrounded, but at least I have a hostage to shield myself with.

"Back off," I shout.

One of the militants steps up, his rifle lowered. The light catches his face: it's Dean.

"Let the kid go, Evans," Dean says.

I blink, realizing I'm restraining a teenager. Patrisse steps up into the doorway of the train, nonchalant. I look at her, and she nods. "Let him go," she says.

Glancing around, I begin to recognize the other militants. Their sunken cheeks, their tired eyes: this is Jackson's team, the one that escorted me from the river. Feeling him tremble in my arms, I release the kid and shove him gently toward his buddies. He turns toward me, rubbing his neck, desperate to keep his composure.

"You're coming with us, Evans," Dean says. "Like it or not."

Patrisse steps down off the train and joins Dean. I look between the two of them. "No," I say. "I'm done here."

"Like hell you are," Dean says. He gestures around at his team. "You've gone and placed targets on all our heads."

Dean tosses me a hand terminal. It's streaming one of the network's news stations. The chyron reads: *Treason, treachery, and now… terrorism.*

I unmute the volume, catching the news anchor mid-report. "Again, breaking news, a Trucast exclusive. We are shocked to report the discovery of a radical-militant terrorist network just miles outside the city limits."

The program cuts to a videotaped statement by President Norton. "My fellow Americans, please," he says, stern. "Though this is a frightening development, one that has escaped our attention until now, please remain calm. Effective immediately, I am placing all metropolitan areas under immediate lockdown until these terrorists can be located and eradicated." Norton softens. "America, we have been through and conquered far greater challenges in our time. War. Socialism. Disease. And we have defeated far greater evils. Believe in me, citizens. For it was I who elevated you out of tragedy before, and it is I who will elevate you once again. Like the great Phoenix…"

I swipe the channel, catching another Trucast news anchor mid-sentence: "… has confirmed that the terrorist network is the brainchild of outlaws Dean and Janice Destin…" Old mugshots of Dean and Janice dissolve onscreen, and my eyes flick toward Dean standing in front of me. He's aged well. "…with their manipulative brainwashing techniques and sadistic leadership, their reach has been far. Included in their ranks: none other than Taylor Evans…"

My face appears onscreen. I snort and swipe to the next channel. "… fearing hundreds dead, authorities are currently searching for survivors…" The program cuts to b-roll of a nursing home… or seemingly what was a nursing home. The building looks to have been demolished. Blood and body parts are strewn about like a horror film.

First responders frantically claw at the rubble, reaching for outstretched hands.

The chyron reads: *Evans destroys nursing home.*

I swipe again, landing on an aerial reconnaissance photograph of the resistance's warehouse. "... in breaking news: the Department of Homeland Security has located their secret training compound in New Jersey..."

I swipe again. Another journalist. "... the National Guard, in conjunction with *The Eagle's Hammer*, has announced a massive offensive..."

I swipe again. This time it's a talk show, the host's face puckered with indignation. "... they're a menace to all upstanding, God-loving Americans, and they must be exterminated. These people, these anarchists: they're rats. They're animals. Kill them all..."

Jamal. All I can think of is Jamal. Is he sleeping on his father's cot? His mother's photos tacked up on the wall next to him? Glimpses of the impending raid flash into my mind: masked nats swarming the compound. Riggs and CJ, smiling sadistically. The panic, confusion, and fear. Then the bloodshed...

"You certainly kicked the hornet's nest," Dean says.

I look at him, then Patrisse. I'm stunned by how quickly the network has spun this. Turning news into propaganda is nothing new. But this, this just happened.

That building, it was abandoned. It wasn't a nursing home. There were no fatalities. There's no doubt that the network's cameras were affixed to that rooftop, capturing the building's destruction live and for all to see. But I think of all the passengers on the subway, scared shitless. I think of the millions of Americans who watched it unfold on live television. Can this country trust its own eyes?

"Come on, Evans," Patrisse says. "Let's go."

CHAPTER 16

A narrow walkway dumps us out beneath the bridge. I look up at the traffic overhead. It's noisy, but at least we're hidden from the recon-drones watching for us.

Stepping to the curb, an old, rust-covered box truck pulls up. We all climb inside the back, finding spots to sit on the floor. Then the door is rolled down and latched, plunging us into darkness.

Instead of marching me back to the compound, Dean and his team are treating me to a ride this time. But this has little to do with pampering Patrisse or me. Time is of the essence. Whatever retaliation the network or the National Guard is planning, the attack is imminent.

Now, you may be asking yourself: what kind of
massacre are these tyrants capable of? The threat increases
significantly depending on who's calling the shots —
whether President Norton or Hanna Hernandez. If it's
Norton, rounding up this resistance and sending them to
re-education camps hits the mark. Most probably won't
survive, and the ones that do will tell stories scary enough to
ward off any copycat dissenters in the future.

But if it's Hernandez calling the shots, God have mercy.
Blood makes for good ratings. And the bloodier, the better.

Dean's hand terminal lights up as he checks the
network's feed. The video casts a flickering illumination
on us all. Avoiding eye contact with me, the ragtag team
is quiet and uneasy. For some of them, this will probably
be their first combat experience. For most of them, it will
certainly be their last.

The truck takes a sharp turn, then accelerates hard.
Seated next to me, Patrisse slides against me. I think about
what she told me: that it wasn't her that saved me. This
means I technically don't owe her anything. Thinking of the
resistance, perhaps I don't owe any of them anything either,
except maybe Jackson — I am wearing his jacket after all.

But my gut tells me otherwise.

I lean toward Patrisse. "Why did you stop and look up at me that day in the lobby?" I ask, whispering to her. "I saw you from above. It was the day...."

"The day you ran, yeah," she says, leaning close enough to me that I can smell her scent. Then she turns to me, her eyes narrowing. "I was looking at you because you disgust me. Everything about you disgusts me."

I stare at her, not sure how to react.

"You won the birth lottery, Evans," she says, biting. "But instead of a golden spoon in your hand, it was a gun. You've never struggled. You've never wanted. You have no idea what it's like to see what little you have slowly slip through your fingers. You've never laid awake in bed and wondered why. Why me? Why this?"

Listening to her, I realize I, too, have had those thoughts. Maybe I'm more of a victim of this fucked up society than she thinks. I recall what childhood memories I do have. And they're horrific: the constant competition between me and the other young hammers; the fear wrapped up in determination; kill or be killed.

I think of Hernandez. I think of myself, just a child, squinting in the studio lights as I looked up at her. I think of the pride I felt when she'd encourage me. But the reward for winning her praise: more blood on my hands.

Hanna Hernandez, I can feel her searching for me now. Like a spotlight sweeping an empty field, I know she will find me eventually. I can run all I want, but this truth weighs heavy on me: I am her monster. There's no escaping that. And there's no forgiving that.

The truck takes another sharp turn, bouncing on potholes and rough pavement. Then it skids to a stop. We're here at the compound. The door slides open, and a chaotic scene greets us. Scared and panicked, evacuees head to the sewer entrance carrying as much food and supplies as possible. Their crying, exhausted children follow behind them.

"I want you splitting into pairs," Dean says, directing the team who rode here with us. "Then escort groups of a dozen or so. Radio in any threats. But keep moving, even when their offensive begins."

"Where are they going?" I ask, asserting myself.

"Wherever," Dean says, glaring at me.

Patrisse turns to see Jackson coming to greet us and smiles. Jamal is in his arms, and as he nears, he sets the kid down and embraces Patrisse. Me, I stand awkwardly nearby, looking anywhere but in their direction. Then I feel a tug at my sleeve. It's Jamal.

"Thank you for saving Patrisse," the kid says.

I nod. "Glad somebody appreciates it," I say.

The four of us follow Dean as he marches into the warehouse, pushing past more frantic evacuees as we enter. The scene inside is as chaotic and urgent as it is outside. Janice is barking orders as we approach, telling people what to take and what to leave.

"Any updates?" Dean asks her.

Janice shakes her head, despondent. "No," she says, "but from the looks of it, we don't have much time."

She points toward a television. Atop Trucast Tower, three helicopters are preparing for take-off. They're heavily modified Sikorskies: military-grade and stealth-equipped. As the support crew runs back and forth, mindful of the rotors, it's all theatrical and cool-looking, but the network is biding its time.

I roll my eyes and turn away — everything's a production.

Another group of evacuees pushes past, their hands full of food supplies, their fear palpable. The compound looks as if a hurricane has ripped through it. What was an impressive make-shift community this morning has already been decimated.

My attention shifts from one familiar face to the next: Janice stacks blankets in a child's arms, patting his head before sending him on his way; Jackson helps a teenage team member with their rifle; checking its action and chambering a round — the kid's probably never fired a weapon in her life; Patrisse comforts Jamal as his world is upended; and Dean grabs two members of his staff, shouting orders...

It all seems so futile... and wrong. But there's no denying it: this is all my fault. I set the actions in motions that have led to this. And maybe it's me who should do something about it.

I look at the white-washed skylight above — rain patters on the glass. I look down at the concrete subfloor and think of the support columns in the basement beneath. And I can visualize it. I can see how it's all going to play out as if I'm watching it on television: the hammer team crashes through the skylight. An intense firefight ensues, with plenty of fireworks. They'll separate us, squaring off one-on-one for our dramatic finales. Patrisse, Jackson, and I — we'll be killed in hand-to-hand combat, all in extreme close-up, all for the world to see, just as Hernandez wants.

"No," I say. "This is wrong."

"Excuse me?" Dean snaps.

"This is a mistake," I say, pointing at Jackson as he's gearing up to leave with a group of evacuees. "*The Eagle's Hammer* is predictable, right? It's the same show night after night. We rush into a home; we find our targets cowering in their bathrooms." I look between Janice, Dean, Jackson, and Patrisse. "The production team, they want it predictable.

Right, Patrisse? It makes the whole thing easier to pull off."
Patrisse shrugs, then nods. "And the network," I continue,
"the network wants spectacle. So, give it to them."

The others stare at me, confused.

"If they want a climactic showdown, let's give it
to them," I say. "They know we're here, and we know
they're coming," I point at the video screen; to the copters
preparing to launch. Then I gesture toward a cluster of
parents carrying their children out in their arms. "They
don't give a shit about them. And hunting them down in
shit-filled sewers, that's boring." I turn to the group. "They
want me. Taylor Evans. They want me in primetime, with
the whole country watching. So, let's give them what they
want: me on a fucking platter."

"That's ridiculous," Janice says, shaking her head. "We
should be defending the escape routes."

"No," Dean says. "He's right."

Jackson and Patrisse, they nod their consent. Janice
looks between us all. She reaches out for Jamal and pulls the
child into her arms, hugging him tightly. "You're going to
get yourselves killed," she says, glaring at us.

"But we're gonna save you," I say.

Patrisse steps up and looks me in the eyes. I'm unsure
what she's thinking or about to say. Then, after a beat, she

reaches into her pocket and pulls out the action figure I had given her to return to Jamal. She stuffs it into my hand.

"Maybe you're a hero after all," she says, then turns and walks away. Me, I catch Jamal peering at me, a hint of adulation in his eyes. *Maybe I am.*

"So, Mister Evans," Dean says, clearing the air. "What exactly do you have in mind?"

I flash a smile. What happens next, you've seen before: it's called a montage. Pick some up-tempo music, maybe something orchestral, and watch me and this ragtag team spring into action.

Me, I'm touring the basement with Dean. I'm checking the structure. And I like what I'm seeing. Patrisse and Jackson, I put them on explosives-detail. Back in the armory, they grab the remaining C-4 explosives... yeah, the same stuff that knocked down that building, nursing home or not. There's plenty of it. Janice, she takes Jamal and heads to safety. The goodbye between the kid and Jackson is enough to make me turn away — who knows if they'll ever see each other again. I see Jackson hand the kid a photo of his mother... heartbreaking shit.

The rest of Dean's team runs about, preparing to fight.

As I said, *The Eagle's Hammer* likes things predictable. The only ace in my hand: being unpredictable. I know what the network expects. I know how they think. To beat them, all I have to do is beat myself. I am their monster, after all — let loose upon themselves.

Me, I can do this. If that makes me a leader, whatever. If this is what I was meant to do, so be it. But that's what I'm going to be: a monster.

Outside, the sound of approaching helicopters grows louder.

"They want a big finish?" I ask the group. "Well, so do I. Now, let's give it to them."

CHAPTER 17

The network fades up on Silas and Skylar in the studio. "Fear not, America," Silas says, his eyes bloodshot and strained. "For the Eagle sees all. The Eagle knows all. And *The Eagle's Hammer...*"

"Is about to drop," they say together.

You, you're transfixed. You and the entire country are glued to your seats, tense and uncertain. It's past your bedtime, it's way past your kid's bedtime, but you've never seen anything like this. And there's no way you'll miss a second of it now.

Tonight, for the first time ever, *The Eagle's Hammer* was fended off on live television for all to see. There's no spinning it any other way. Taylor Evans, who just days ago was their celebrated leader, the public face of the team and all they represent, has turned on them. And he's proving to be as deadly fighting against them as he was murdering for them.

Now, in coordination with the National Guard, *The Eagle's Hammer* is on the cusp of raiding an until-now secret terrorist training facility just outside of town. But you can't help but take pause with such a development: how the hell had that gone undiscovered until now?

You, you can't even blow through a tollbooth without the nats knocking on your door... or worse yet, the hammer. And yet, there's a terrorist training facility... in New Jersey?

Mixed within all this wall-to-wall news coverage are cheeky little reminders that, despite reports of fringe social media chatter claiming that the building destroyed wasn't actually a nursing home — any discussions or attempts to propagate such fake news to undermine authorities are illegal. But these moments, if anything, appear to be cracks in the network's armor, making the whole experience that much more engrossing.

Now, those Sikorsky helicopters are en route. And you're overcome with nervous anticipation, unsure of what to expect or who to root for.

The broadcast cuts to a live shot inside the lead copter. The three hammers are strapped in and ready to rock. For this special occasion, they've got on fresh duds and a sleek alternative helmet-armor combo. Milner stands over the pilot's shoulder, eyeing their approach. From up here, the warehouse is a pathetic sight.

Milner turns to the other hammers and clears his throat. "Okay, hammers," he says, grabbing their attention. He holds up a display pad for the team and camera to see. On its screen is an infrared satellite feed of the structure. "The terrorists are here," Milner shouts, pointing at the red blob at the center — our heat signatures. "Any questions?"

Gorman shakes his head. "We're ready, sir," he says.

Riggs pumps a fist. "Let's fuck 'em up," she says.

"Yeah," CJ says, the camera zooming in to a close-up of him. "Let's hammer 'em good."

"In position," Milner yells. The hammers unbuckle from their seats and stand. Carrying their deployment bags in one hand and their assault rifles in the other, they shuffle toward the door. As Milner slides it open, the wind swirls around them.

"Hold there," Riley says in Milner's ear. Back at the second helicopter, two dozen hover-cams deploy and zip into position. "Alright. It's all you, buddy," Riley says, content. "Take it away."

Milner clips his deployment bag to the copter and peers at their target below. As the camera gets in his face — and the music swells — he stands square-jawed and stoic. You, you at home: you know exactly what's coming...

"It's showtime," Milner says, delivering his classic catchphrase without missing a beat. And then he jumps.

CUT TO: The white-washed skylight as the team smashes through it, repelling from the copter above. The shattered glass and twisted metal frame fall to the floor, followed quickly by hover-cams. The hammers land on their feet, guns blazing. Their barrage of gunfire destroys everything in sight.

You, you watch as the hideout — the temporary hospital, the makeshift school and chapel, the personal cots and tents — it's all blown to pieces. Stuffed animals, first aid kits, vegetable gardens — they're shredded mercilessly. Brass shell casings fly through the air, and blue gun smoke fills the space. The devastation is thorough, and the hammers, they love every second of it.

Finally, with a closed fist, Milner orders them to cease fire. But as the dust settles and the smoke clears, they're left dumbfounded and confused. Riggs looks left, then right. Then she looks behind herself, bumping into CJ.

"Fucking place is empty," she shouts, not waiting for direction from the network.

"No shit," Gorman says, frustrated.

At home, you breathe a sigh of relief.

Milner's eyes narrow as he takes it in. "What's the story?" he whispers to the production crew.

"Standby," Riley says. "Refreshing your data feed."

In Milner's helmet, his display updates, overlaying the infrared heat signatures. From the looks of it, they're standing right on top of them. Milner looks around, then down. "For fuck's sake," he says, staring at the floor. "There's a basement…"

Me, I've been watching the broadcast on Dean's hand terminal the whole time. Satisfied with the panic on Milner's face, I turn to Patrisse and give her a thumbs up. She pushes the munitions detonator in her lap, then covers her head…

BOOM. BOOM. BOOM.

A series of isolated explosions take out the subfloor's support columns, demolition style. The collapse is almost instant. The entire cement center of the building, including Milner and the hammer team, pancakes to the basement… where I'm sitting and waiting.

Now, how's that for spectacle?

On my cue, Jackson, Dean, and a handful of Dean's team open fire. Bullets tear into the hammers, their armor absorbing most of the slugs. Rounds ricochet off their helmets as they scurry for cover.

"It's a fucking ambush," Riggs yells, diving behind a large chunk of concrete.

"Ah, fuck this," CJ says, plucking a grenade from his vest and lobbing it. It lands near us and detonates. But Patrisse and Jackson are first-rate combatants who return suppression fire immediately. Watching Patrisse, the girl can handle a weapon. And she looks good using it too...

Zeroing in on our positions, CJ lobs another grenade. And then another. I can't say he's aiming for anybody in particular, but the blasts are enough to scatter us. The hammers use the disruption to scramble to the perimeter. With drones buzzing over our heads, our advantage has been effectively minimized.

As for Milner, scanning the scene through the wafting smoke, I've lost eyes on him... Damn. "Fall back!" I shout.

With hover-cams in tow, CJ and Riggs flank the nearest, inexperienced resistance fighter — he's just a kid. Emptying his clip, the kid tries to run, but it's too late. CJ is on him like a wild animal, snapping his neck with his bare hands. Riggs loves it. She howls with delight before laying down more cover fire.

Patrisse and I leap behind another pillar. Jackson scrambles over to us. "Their armor's too much," he shouts.

"We've got to move on them, or it's game over," Patrisse says, nodding.

Jackson looks at me. "Any suggestions?"

I consider. "It's me they're after. But they'll draw it out and milk the ratings," I say. "You two fall back to the control center. Make some commotion and draw their fire. I'll bring up the rear."

Patrisse smiles. "You're using us as bait, aren't you?" I hesitate, then nod. Patrisse laughs. "Let's go, Jackson," she says, slapping him on the shoulder. They hurry along the perimeter.

Me, I head the other way. I can hear Riggs out there somewhere, cackling. I turn a corner, watching the hover-cams overhead, when I hear my name...

"Evans! Watch your back!"

A shot rings out, and I spin around. Gorman takes the bullet and stumbles behind cover. He'd been tracking me like a pro, and I had no idea. I turn back to find Dean, gun in hand — he totally saved my ass.

"Amateur, Evans," Dean says. "Real amateur." He and a pair of his team clamber over concrete rubble to my position. "What's our situation?"

"Dire," I say, flashing a smile. "As expected. Get you and your team out of here, Dean. They did good."

He nods, then gives me a look. "Stay alive, Evans," he says, extending his hand. We shake, and then he's off.

Me, I head toward Gorman. Leaning against the pillar he jumped behind, I follow his trail of blood around it. And that's where I find him: clutching his injured shoulder and cursing profusely — Dean's bullet caught him right between two armored plates.

Gorman's eyes flick up in my direction. He leaps for his rifle, but I kick it away, keeping mine leveled at his gut.

"Shit," Gorman sighs.

Eying the drones, we're not the focus of the broadcast's attention... yet. But I should milk this moment with Gorman to give Dean and company time to hit the sewers and escape. I fire a volley of gunshots into the air toward the hover-cams — that should do the trick.

They want a show, I'll give them one.

Gorman and I slowly sidestep each other, smoke wafting between us. Nervous and jittery, I realize Gorman is scared to death.

"Come on, Gorman," I say. "You're more scared than most of our targets."

"Don't kill me, Evans," he says, keeping tabs on the drones. "I never wanted this. I never wanted to kill people, and certainly not you."

I lower my weapon. Could he be telling the truth? I glance at the cameras — they're still far enough away to not pick up what we're saying.

"Take me with you," Gorman says. "Let's get out of here, together. Fuck this shit. Fuck Milner and Hernandez."

"Bullshit," I say, testing him, raising my weapon again.

"Wait," he says, his eyes darting toward the hover-cams, mindful of their proximity. "Wait, Evans," he says, changing his approach. "Look. You have no idea what's going on. You don't have a clue. It's all bullshit."

I blink. "What are you saying, Gorman?"

His eyes meet mine. "It's all bullshit. This. The resistance. It's all a part of the show."

I stare at him, stunned. A hover-cam approaches us, its tiny propellers spinning the smoke around it, and Gorman steels himself. Any window of communication we just had, has closed. But me, I'm not playing the game anymore. If I could call a time-out, I would.

"What the hell are you talking about, Gorman?" I ask.

But Gorman pulls his pistol. Reflexively, I lunge for his wrist. BAM. A shot rings out, but I've pushed the barrel away. I twist behind him, and we drop to our knees, straining against each other.

"Gorman…" I say.

"Fuck you, Evans," Gorman says.

BAM. Another shot rings out: Gorman is desperate. BAM. He squeezes off another. The hover-cam inches toward us, a nice dramatic push-in. BAM. Another shot rings out. Then another. BAM. Gorman growls as I pull the gun toward him until it's snug beneath his chin, pressing against his flesh.

"Gorman," I say, whispering to him. "Please…"

"Fuck… you…. Evans," he says, his teeth clenched.

He was toying with me, right? I had him boxed in; he had no chance… so he tried confusing me to buy himself more time. I let my guard down, just like he wanted. Another hover-cam sweeps into position near us, and I know you're watching at home; you're all watching…

"Gorman," I say. "Please…"

The cameras are circling us so close I feel their propeller wash on my face. Gorman's arm shakes in my hands, his eyes wide and panicked. I've seen this look before, thousands of times. The acceptance of one's imminent death. His whole body begins to buck — and then he goes limp…

He's given up. I don't even think I'm the one holding the gun to his head anymore…

"Don't," I say, realizing what's coming next. "Gorman, don't!"

BAM. Gorman pulls the trigger and blows his brains out. Up and out, just like Milner coached us. Up and out toward the drones watching us. His body collapses in my arms, and I'm left speechless and stunned.

What the fuck just happened?

CHAPTER 18

Riggs' laugh cuts through the cacophony, and I drop
Gorman's now lifeless body. Whatever he said — whatever
nonsense he was buying time with — I push it far out of
my mind. I don't have time for that, not right now.

Peeking over the rubble that was the first floor of the
warehouse, I spot Patrisse and Jackson executing the plan
flawlessly. Together, they're skillfully luring Riggs and
CJ toward the control center. Even the hover-cams are
converging on that location, eager for action.

With the trap set, I carefully work my way along the
perimeter as Patrisse lays down cover fire for Jackson.
Jackson darts into the room, then Patrisse follows him.
Riggs and CJ pop up, guns blazing. Their barrage shatters

the glass separating the area, but Patrisse and Jackson slide safely behind the server racks.

"Come on out, you bitch," Riggs shouts, then laughs. In a well-rehearsed approach, Riggs and CJ methodically work their way closer and closer.

Patrisse, glancing out, spots me bringing up the rear, closing the box. Our eyes meet — those beautiful eyes — and she nods. It's my show now.

Riggs and CJ are just outside the control center, peeking in and sizing up the room. Patrisse opens fire in their direction, letting her clip run empty. "Shit," she says, loud enough for all to hear — all part of the ploy.

Riggs snickers. "You've made a big mistake scurrying in there," she says as she and CJ inch into the room, the glass crunching beneath their feet. A pair of hover-cams sweep ahead, setting up their shots. Feeling confident, Riggs and CJ stand, then round the corner...

That's when I chamber a round.

Riggs and CJ spin toward me.

"Shit," CJ says, knowing they're fucked.

Me, I open fire, chasing them with bullets as they dive for the far corner of the room. They duck behind a counter as I pound the area, destroying the video screens and office chairs.

"Son of a bitch," CJ shouts, crawling deeper into the maze of servers and equipment racks. He draws his handgun and blindly squeezes off a round at me.

Me, I continue my advance. Inching closer, I pull a grenade from my vest and show it to Patrisse and Jackson...

Two birds with one stone. But as I'm about to pull the pin and send it rolling, a voice booms from behind me: "Not so fast, Evans."

It's Milner — I had forgotten all about him. I turn to see him approaching, dragging Jamal along, whimpering. Jackson springs out from his hiding spot, weapon raised.

"Let him go," Jackson shouts, desperate to save his son. Patrisse grabs Jackson and holds him back. "You son of a bitch, let him go!"

Milner smiles triumphantly as the cameras circle him — the spotlight is all his. He brings his pistol to Jamal's temple, and the child starts to cry.

"Drop your weapons," Milner says. "All of you."

Patrisse and I exchange a quick glance, but what can we do? We toss our weapons to the ground, Jackson too. Janice steps out from behind Milner, her hands raised and whimpering.

"I'm sorry," she says, staring at Jackson. "He caught us in the sewer..."

"Shut up," Milner snaps. Janice closes her eyes, trembling. Milner shoves her and Jamal forward into the control center. Spotting Riggs and CJ hiding beneath the counter, Milner shakes his head. "Round 'em up," he shouts.

Riggs and CJ crawl out and compose themselves. Riggs swings her rifle at me, directing me to join Patrisse and Jackson. "Hands above your heads," she shouts, still embarrassed. "Now line the wall. All of you."

We do as we're told, Janice and Jamal too. But as the kid approaches his father, he breaks into a sprint.

"You little shit!" Riggs shouts, grabbing Jamal by the collar. She lifts him off the ground, his feet hanging beneath him.

Jackson lunges toward her, but CJ grabs him by the neck with one hand, then decks him across the face with his other. The blow knocks Jackson back, and he spits blood.

Riggs lets loose with one of her hyena cackles.

Me, I'm uneasy about the way she's holding Jamal — like he's not even human. "If you hurt that kid," I say, glaring at her.

"You'll what, Evans?" she barks back at me, rifle leveled at my chest. I stare at her, unflinching. Finally, Riggs shakes her head with disgust. "You're pathetic."

She tosses Jamal at Jackson like he's a rag doll. Jackson barely manages to catch him, but he does. The father and son embrace. "It's okay, baby," Jackson says, cradling Jamal. "I've got you, bud. I've got you."

"Against the wall," Riggs says.

She forces Jackson to turn and shoves him and Jamal into the cinder blocks. Janice and I follow along. CJ steps forward, and I realize how fucked we are. Janice, she had one job: get the kid out of here. Now he's going to die with the rest of us. I close my eyes, exasperated.

"How's it feel, Evans?" CJ asks, right behind me. I feel his breath hot on my neck. The hover-cams position themselves around the two of us. Shot, reverse-shot. "How's it feel being on the receiving end of the hammer?"

I think of the production crew anticipating my reaction. I picture Riley back in Trucast Tower, waiting impatiently. And I picture Hernandez up on the Eight-Four, her eyes glued to the screen as a bottle of champagne chills in anticipation. They all want something from me.

But then I picture you; you in your l-iving room, your family surrounding you: you want something from me too. Maybe it's me begging for forgiveness. Or perhaps it's a smart-ass retort. But I give neither — it's a fill-in-the-blank moment of emotion.

CJ unsheathes his knife and places the cold, steel blade against my neck. "Scared, Evans?" CJ asks. "How about a shave?"

He drags the blade's edge against my skin, cutting me slightly. I don't cringe, but I do close my eyes. Facing death: this is something new to me. My pulse, I feel it racing; I feel my heart begging me to flee. But here I am, out of options… even bad ones.

I laugh at the ridiculousness of it all.

CJ and Riggs, they glance at each other, then CJ shoves me into the wall. "What's so funny, Evans?"

"You," I say. "You're not going to kill me, CJ. They won't give a dumbass like you the glory." I eye him behind me. "The ratings, the celebrity, you won't get it. You're just too stupid. And ugly too." My eyes dart at Riggs. "You either, Riggs. Neither of you is star-material, and you know it. You're barely second rate." I shake my head and look straight at the wall again. "No, the kill will go to Milner. Or, better yet, I'll be dragged back to Trucast Tower. Cause the network is going to milk this. Because, here's the thing." I glance back at them, making sure they're listening. "Even as a treasonous, hammer-murdering traitor, I'll still get better ratings than you two blow-hards ever will."

CJ and Riggs blink, both stunned silent. But the hover-cams are waiting for their reactions — they have to do something.

"Shut up," CJ says, slamming my face into the wall. "You might be right," he sneers. "You might walk out of here alive… but that doesn't mean your friends will."

CJ snickers as he steps down the line, looking each of us over. Since we're hopelessly standing here against the wall, let me tell you about this guy. He's been a hammer as long as me. And in that span, I haven't met a more vile person. One time, the team and I, we were in a target's home. It was Chicago or Cincinnati. Somewhere like that. And as soon as we smashed down the front door and stomped inside, there were kittens. Four or five of them, meowing at our feet. Now, you don't see cats anymore. You don't see dogs. Not since food became so expensive. But this person, our target, had a whole litter.

We went about our business. Sticking to the script, we said our lines and killed our target. But on the way out, CJ couldn't help but stop at these kittens. He bent down and picked one up. This adorable little ball of fur, he held it up for us to see… and then he twisted that cat's head off like a bottle cap. Then he did it again. And again… four or five times.

And Riggs, she just laughed. Just like she's laughing now. That's CJ for you. And Riggs too. Thank God we're in a commercial break, or he might be twisting Jamal's head off right now.

As he lingers behind us, his knife at the ready, I look at Patrisse. This woman, she's full of surprises: like when she kicked the explosives into the belly of that building. She's fearless. Damned if she knew how that building would fall, let alone whether we'd survive. But she had a wild card and wasn't afraid to play it. Now, with CJ lining up for a kill, I can't help but wonder: does she have anything else up her sleeve?

"Butterscotch," Patrisse says to me.

I blink. "What?" A smirk grows on her face as her eyes brighten. She nods at me. "Butterscotch?" I ask, saying the word louder this time, loud enough to be overheard.

CJ and Riggs exchange a confused look. "What the hell did you say, Evans?" Riggs asks. Stepping up to me, she pulls her handgun and places it on the back of my head.

Me, my eyes are still locked with Patrisse. She smiles and winks. "Butterscotch," she mouths silently.

I peer back at the gun to my head. What do I have to lose? "Butterscotch," I say, loud and clear.

CJ and Riggs hesitate. I see their eyes gloss over as they shift their attention to the voice in their ears: Riley.

"What the hell does that mean?" Riley asks, having lost his patience. "Butterscotch," he says, repeating it for all the crew to hear. "Can somebody please tell me what the hell that's supposed to…"

Patrisse, she drops to the ground, straight down. Jackson and Janice follow her lead, covering their and Jamal's head. Me, I look at them stunned until Patrisse drags me down too, laughing.

That's when it happens…

Butterscotch.

When spoken aloud by Riley back in the control room, that word, all the way back in Trucast Tower, triggers a maliciously little computer worm buried deep in each of the hover-units programming. This worm was dormant until this moment — when Patrisse and the resistance would need it the most. It's so fucking clever, it's poetic.

At the sound of that word, each hover-cam circling us stops dead in its tracks, processing the voice command it just received. And then, acquiring their new targets — *the hammers* — and their new instructions — *to attack* — it begins…

The chaos is beautiful. The first camera slams into Riggs, taking her by surprise. It's a devastating blow that knocks the wind out of her. She keels over when another drone, with considerable speed, smashes into her visor, knocking her off her feet.

"The fuck is this?" CJ asks, swinging his rifle up. But a drone knocks the weapon right out of his hand. Two more zip toward him. He drops to his knees, but it isn't enough: the hover-cams sandwich him.

From the floor, I watch two more drones pelt CJ in quick succession as he retreats under the counter. He pulls out his handgun and lets loose, but the drones are moving too fast to pick off. Milner takes a few shots, then dives for cover.

Like I said: it's beautiful.

Me, I glance at Patrisse. I am thoroughly impressed. This is her; this is all her. She must have spent years on this. With access to the production equipment, she must have systematically embedded this worm into the hover-unit A.I. programming. Since the drones react in real-time to Riley's voice commands, the key was using a word unlikely to be spoken. With Patrisse's technical know-how, I'm sure it was easy too.

When I knocked on her door, no wonder she was burning those hard drives and devices on her living room floor. She was destroying the evidence.

A hover-cam buzzes above us. And then another one. They're not aiming for us; they're targeting the hammers. Riggs, CJ, and Milner — it might be their geolocators. The same data the programming uses to compose nice and dramatic closeups of the hammers is now being used to calculate kamikaze attacks.

"Come on," I shout to the others. "Let's go!"

Patrisse takes Janice's hand, and we run. With Jamal in his arms, Jackson follows as we flee the control center.

Milner, he chases after us. "Stop!" he shouts, only to be tagged by a drone. Milner falls to the ground but manages to dodge another attack. As the hover-cam circles back for another approach, Milner aims.

BAM — he blasts it out of the air.

"Evans," Milner shouts, standing up.

BAM — he takes out another one.

Me and the others, we don't stop running. We approach the stairs, and I stop to help Janice and Patrisse over the rubble. Jackson and Jamal too. I eye Milner as he follows us, swinging at hover-cams like they're houseflies. He's fast but not fast enough. A drone ricochets off him, sliding into the ground.

BAM — he finishes it.

"Keep moving," I shout, charging up the stairs. We hurry to the nearest exit.

BAM. BAM. More gunshots ring out from the basement as I meet up with Patrisse and the others at the door. Patrisse is looking out through the tarp, concerned.

"What is it?" I ask.

"The copters, they're still here," she says. I glance back the way we came, then look at Jackson. He shrugs.

"The sewers are our only chance, man," Jackson says.

One of the copters roars overhead, its spotlight sweeping the opening as it waits for us to make our move. The noise is deafening, and Jamal cries into his father's chest.

"Fuck," I say, glancing back toward the stairs. Milner is on his way. "We've got to make a run for it. Wait for my cue."

I dart outside, run a few meters, then stop. The spotlight locks on me; then the entire copter turns toward me. "Okay!" I shout to the others. "Go! Go! Go!"

Patrisse and Janice sprint by me, but the spotlight stays on me — I'm the one they want. Jackson runs for it, but he slips in the mud.

"Jackson, hurry," I shout, watching him helplessly.

Low to the ground, the copter is only a few hundred feet away. I can see the Gatling gun rotate and aim. Any second now, they're going to light me up…

Automatic fire rings out, but not at me. It's coming from atop the box truck that drove us here. I turn to see Dean standing atop it, machine gun in hand.

The slugs pockmark the copter's fuselage, and it peels off. Patrisse and Janice cheer from the entrance of the sewer.

Me, I look back at Jackson. He and Jamal are all smiles as they rush toward me. But my focus shifts past them, toward the entrance of the compound. Milner steps into the frame, pistol in hand. He takes aim…

"Jackson, no!" I leap toward them…

BAM.

CHAPTER 19

The bullet hits me, lodging in my shoulder. The pain is unlike anything I have ever experienced, and I fall. Just like in a movie, everything goes quiet and muffled as I fade in and out of consciousness. One second I'm here, face-first in mud, as a squadron of helicopters converges on my position. The next, I'm far away, strapped in the scramjet as it streaks toward another city — me, I'm fully prepared to kill another target.

I'm in again. Milner stares at me, gun in hand, smoke still rising from the barrel. Dean, atop the box truck, spots him. He swings his rifle toward him and opens fire. But Milner scrambles back inside the warehouse just in time.

The copters, they lock on Dean. And an air-to-surface missile streaks toward him…

KA-BOOM.

Fire engulfs Dean and the truck, and the explosion blows them to pieces. Janice, I hear her screaming — her husband has just been killed, right in front of her. Patrisse picks up and cradles Jamal in her arms as Jackson drags me into the sewer.

"Leave me," I mumble. "Let me die."

I was twenty-four years old when I got my first kill. I'd been on the team for three years at that point. The youngest member. The heartthrob. Milner, he was lead-hammer at the time. And he wasn't happy, even then, sharing the spotlight. But Milner was due for retirement, and the network had high hopes for me. Only Joaquin had doubts; he argued that I wasn't ready and needed more time. But Hernandez had made up her mind.

The target was my age. Twenty-four. But our lives, they were lightyears apart. Her name? I have no idea. I couldn't be bothered to remember, even then. Her crime? Who knows. Her eyes were brown. Big and brown. And, as the hover-cams circled us, she begged for mercy. But I held my handgun to her forehead and pulled the trigger, just as I was directed to do. Never once did I question the ethics of what

I was doing. It didn't faze me, not in the least. This woman, my age and desperate to live, was nothing to me nor society.

Shit. Shit is everywhere, floating on the water's surface, disgusting and vile. Jackson is dragging me through the dark, cold sewers. The shit is in my wound. Patrisse is in the lead. Me, I have no idea where we are or why. But this is nothing new. My whole life, I've been led by others. I've been told what to do and when to do it. All without batting an eye.

"Let me die," I mumble. "Just let me die."

We're up on the surface in a dark alley, hiding between over-filled dumpsters. Rats and filth. A good place to die. A car cruises along the road, and we hold our breath until it passes — not a nat patrol. Not this time.

Patrisse pounds on a metal door. No answer. She pounds again. A series of deadbolts and latches unlock. The door opens. And a pair of masked gunmen greet us with silent stares. Me, I'm eying the Chinese knock-off sub-machine guns in their hands — what a sorry excuse for weaponry.

"We have nowhere else to go," Patrisse says.

The two men are reluctant, but they let us inside.

Me, I'm thinking about Milner. I'm thinking how he doesn't miss, not at that range, not with that gun. No,

Milner is still playing his game. Which means the network still wants me alive.

Milner, I see him standing in a pool of light at the training facility. He's grinning at me. "Clock's ticking," he says. "A good hammer always finds their way home."

Me, I'm backing away from him with growing dread. But it's not him I'm afraid of. *It's them.* And I know with absolute certainty, they've found me...

"Find your way home," Milner says. But suddenly, Milner isn't Milner — he's my first victim, a hole blown out the back of her head. "Find your way home," she says. And then, from behind her, steps another of my victims. Then another. "Find your way home," they say in unison. "Find your way home."

The lights in the facility fade up: and I'm surrounded. Every target I ever killed is here, reaching for me. With their faces drooped and eyes glossed over, they inch toward me.

"Find your way home," they say. "Find your way home."

And I am terrified.

Patrisse, she slaps me awake. I'm laying on a cot, with just about everybody — the masked gunmen included — standing around me, watching. Patrisse tells me they have to remove the bullet from my shoulder. She tells me I'm septic.

"This is going to hurt," she says.

Jackson holds me down as the pliers go in. Me, I'm kicking and screaming. It's a pain I couldn't have imagined; pain no human should endure. And then they're all there — my victims — enjoying my misery. Each of them, smiling and nodding, they're cheering this torture on.

Justice? Is this justice? No, I should be dead. They're here to drag me to hell. But not yet, it's not time yet.

At the height of the pain, when I fear it may break me, I feel a cool, comforting touch against my skin. I look, and it's Jamal; he's taken my hand. He's comforting me, and I stare at him, thankful.

It's just me and him, peaceful and serene.

The slug drops to the floor. And I'm out…

The year was 1946. The war was over. And the Nuremberg Trials had reached its conclusion. But as the verdicts were read, Hermann Göring — the highest-ranking Nazi official still alive — sat there smiling as if he knew something the world did not. Göring was an alluring and charismatic persona whom people gravitated toward, even while imprisoned by the allied forces. As he heard his sentencing — execution by hanging — Göring sat there smirking. *Like it was all a game.* He sat there, glancing between the spectators and cameras, smiling…

Me, I'm reminded of Hanna Hernandez. I see her smiling like it's all a game. I see her with a crystal flute in hand, the champagne bubbling. Göring managed to kill himself the night before his execution. Somebody had snuck him in a capsule of cyanide. But his twelve underlings, they still went to the gallows. No wonder he was smiling.

My eyes flutter open. Patrisse and one of the masked men lean over me. They're applying a synthetic polymer to my wound — pretty sophisticated stuff to have on hand here, but it'll increase my recovery time exponentially.

The guy notices I'm awake. "Guess you're gonna live after all," he says, shrugging. "Oh well."

A television is on, tuned to one of the network's many channels. I don't see it, but I hear it. On the air now, a pundit is talking at length. "... shouldn't feel guilty about these patrols. Rounding up dissidents is fundamental to American society, as patriotic as the Pledge of Allegiance. I mean, re-education is in the Bible, after all. It's not called that by name, no. But it's there. It's the teaching of Christ, right? And as for those, you know, too far gone. Too radicalized. Well, that's why we have *The Eagle's Hammer*, isn't it? They take evil off this Earth, just as God intended. And it is a righteous thing that they do, the American way..."

The channel changes. Now it's a street interview. An average citizen plucked from a crowd nervously gives their opinion on a subject. ".... I feel safer, personally. I mean, I'm not a criminal or an anarchist or anything like that. So yeah, rounding them up or... or hammering them... yeah, it's a good thing. I don't want... those people shouldn't exist. They have no right to exist..."

The channel changes again, landing on a daytime talk show. My ears perk up at the sound of Candis's voice, my wife. "... this ordeal has been incredibly tough," she says, sobbing. "It's been a nightmare." Candis pauses to collect herself.

"Go ahead," an interviewer says. "Tell America the truth. They deserve it."

"Yes," Candis says, taking a deep breath. "It's just that, Taylor was..." her voice trembles. "Taylor was a tyrant. He demanded complete control of my life. Who I talked to, what I did. It was... it was hell." She begins sobbing. "And he was... merciless. He would... beat me. He would yell and hit me. He was a monster. A monster..."

I'm out again, and the elevator doors open to the Eight-Four. Hernandez slithers toward me, then hands me my own glass of champagne. "Do you hear them?" she asks, smiling. "They love you."

I hear nothing. Not at first. Then I hear chanting.

"Evans. Evans. Evans."

Hernandez leads me to the windows, and we look out. Above us, helicopters circle. Via megaphones, they shout threats to disperse... or else. On the street below, a mass of people is amidst a violent riot. The street fronts are smashed, and cars are flipped over; burning patrol cars are sprinkled among them. Smoke and teargas intermix and waft toward us. The mob, they're attacking the entrance of the tower, trying to force their way inside.

Hernandez giggles. "Isn't it beautiful?" she asks, clinking her flute with mine.

The crowd continues their chant: "Evans. Evans. Evans."

Me, I stare down at them and wonder how they'll kill us. Will they hang us? Firing squad? Or will they simply bludgeon us to death here atop Trucast Tower?

I delight in the possibilities...

"Run, Evans, run!" Jamal says.

The kid is at the foot of my bed, playing with his action figures on the cot. I can barely focus my eyes, but I ask who's who. This one is him, he says, holding up a green-colored hero. This one is daddy, he says, holding up a blue-colored figure. And this one is you, Jamal says, holding up the action figure he had given me before.

I nod, happy to see that the toy survived the raid on the compound. Liking that, I watch the battle unfold, wondering if the good guys will win. Jamal, Jackson, and me: it's the three of us versus the world.

I'm out again. Somewhere bright. A breeze on my face, the wind in the trees: the playground. My dream, this is my dream. I look at my hands: they're adult hands. I touch my face. It's my face. I'm a grownup, not a child. I hear laughter over my shoulder, and I turn toward the playset. Is it Jamal?

But the playground is empty.

I think of the woman, my mother. I look for her. But before I see her, I hear her. "What have you done?" she asks.

I turn and find her approaching me cautiously. Seeing her, I'm relieved and happy. I want to hug her, embrace her — my mother. But the woman, she glares at me.

"What have you done?" she repeats.

I shrug, speechless. Then, stepping out from behind the trees and swing set, I spot them: my victims. They've found me, even here in the park.

Tears well up in my mother's eyes. "You're a monster," she says, jabbing a finger at me. My victims, in all their violent gore, they come to her side.

"A monster," they say as if it's a prayer response.

"Why?" my mother asks. "Why would you do this? Why would you do this to us?"

And I realize there is now a gun in my hand. But I have no control over it. All on its own, as if controlled by some unseen force, my arm levels the pistol at my mother. I shake my head, but I can't stop it. There's nothing I can do. I can't speak. I can't breathe. I am frozen.

You put a weapon in my hand and…

"You're a monster," she says, staring me in the eyes.

"A monster," my victims repeat.

"Please," I manage to blurt out. "Please make it stop…"

BAM.

CHAPTER 20

I startle awake, finding myself in the same room I've been recovering in for days. But considering I can see and think clearly, it seems my fever has broken.

My shoulder hurts. The muscles are tight, and the skin is constrictive. But it's manageable, and I sit up. Rubbing the sleep out of my eyes, I hear voices on the other side of the door. I swing my feet off the cot and wobble out of the room and into the green-blue fluorescent light of an old automotive garage.

I take in the surroundings. Old vehicles — some gas-powered, others autonomous EVs — are in various stages of repair. With boarded-up and blacked-out windows, the space has more of an air of criminality than a legitimate business venture. In all likelihood, this place is a chop shop.

Patrisse, Jackson, and Janice are seated at a rickety table, mugs of coffee in their hands. Jamal, he's on top of a blanket on the floor, playing with his action figures. Of the four, he's the only one to greet me with a smile. The masked gunmen, fortunately, are nowhere to be seen.

Me, I can't tell if I've interrupted a discussion or if this lot is now permanently frazzled. The latter would not surprise me, especially after the assault on the compound. Not to mention Dean's demise…

I turn to Janice. "I'm sorry for your loss," I say.

Janice nods, then offers me a chair. I hobble over and sit. Patrisse eyes me. "How you feeling?" she asks.

"Light-headed but good," I say, checking my shoulder. "This is impressive work. You'd make a good medic."

Patrisse shrugs. "I'll add it to my résumé."

Sitting in silence, I can't help but replay our last moments at the warehouse: Milner shooting me, the approaching helicopters, Dean's heroics, then the explosion. If they had left me, Dean might still be alive. But instead, they dragged me away.

I didn't ask for that. I didn't ask for any of this. But… I can't help but feel appreciative. Despite the years of our comradery, no hammer would have ever sacrificed themselves for me. And certainly not Milner.

I clear my throat. "Thank you," I say, glancing between the three at the table. I look at Jamal seated on the floor. "You too, little man."

The kid smiles and nods.

Through the nearest garage door, we hear a vehicle approach. I glance at the others, gauging their alarm. They're uncertain but stay seated. Footsteps approach the door. The locks unlatch, and the two men enter, armed and still masked. One comes to the table while the other locks the door behind them.

Me, I watch the man limp. Judging by how he drags that leg, I bet it was a gunshot.

"What is it?" Patrisse asks.

The gunmen glance uneasily at each other, then at me.

"There's something you should see," the one says.

"The news broke about an hour ago," the other says, limping toward an old television. He turns on the screen, and it flickers to life. We watch as Milner and Candis appear, facing each other on a pompous and bright set. The sound is muted, but Candis nods as Milner's mouth flaps — he must be a guest on Candis's show.

Then a photo dissolves on-screen: it's a decades-old profile picture of a woman. The woman is young and smiling. But then I recognize her: this is the woman from my dreams. This woman is my mother. Then I notice the chyron graphic along the bottom of the screen, explaining the situation: *Taylor Evans' Mother Arrested.*

My jaw drops, stunned. The others, they shoot me quizzical looks. "Volume," I say, choking on the words. "Turn it up."

Staring at me, it takes the gunman a moment to snap from his daze. He jabs the volume button on the side of the television. Patrisse and Jackson, they glance uneasily at each other as Milner's voice fills the room mid-sentence.

"... nothing wrong with her arrest," Milner says. "Unorthodox, certainly. But these are unorthodox times. The thing to remember here is this: Taylor Evans has committed treason. He's a traitor. An enemy of the state." The program cuts to a reaction shot of Candis. She dabs at the tears in her eyes with a tissue but nods in agreement. "He's defiled everything that makes this country so great, so prosperous," Milner continues, smug. "And quite frankly, his mother: she deserves to die for giving birth to this monster…"

I look between the others at the table. Janice reaches for my hand. "I'm sorry, Taylor," she says, comforting me.

But I pull away, still dumbfounded.

Patrisse turns to me. "Is she your mother?" she asks, doubtful.

"Next channel," I say, ignoring her. But Patrisse's question hangs in the air. "Next channel," I snap.

The screen flickers to the next channel where we find footage of last night's raid being re-aired. It looks like any other Eagle's Hammer broadcast: the team, led by Milner, kicks down the front door. They storm inside, guns drawn. They find the woman cowering in the bathroom — it's always the bathroom.

"Evans," Patrisse says. "Is that your mother?"

"I don't know," I say, unable to look away from the footage. As they drag her out, I'm stunned by how familiar the woman is. She's older than in my dreams. Two or three decades. Her hair is grey, wrinkles around her eyes.

She's terrified — a look I know all too well. Her features: her cheekbones, her chin. Yeah, we could be related. But me, here at the table, I can't process this. The fact that this woman actually exists shatters me.

I look at Patrisse, then Janice, the anguish on my face saying it all. "Is she?" I ask.

Janice shifts in her chair. "Hard to say," she says. "All medical records, your birth certificate, they were destroyed when you entered the hammer program..."

But I raise a hand, silencing her.

"I recognize her," I say.

Patrisse eyes me critically. She leans onto the table as if interrogating a witness. "How?" she asks. "All your memories, they were wiped…."

"My dreams," I say. "I've seen this woman in my dreams."

Patrisse laughs. "The memories you do have, these dreams, they're implants," she says. "They're standard psych-op protocols to keep you in line." I flash her a cold glare. "Let me guess," Patrisse says. "You have these dreams when you're upset or emotional. You have these dreams when you can't believe how much of a nightmare killing innocent people on national television, night after night, actually is."

I say nothing. Patrisse looks me over. "You were just dreaming about her now, weren't you?" she asks.

Again, I stay silent. Fuck this shit.

Patrisse shakes her head. "I'm sorry," she says. "This is all standard manipulation. To keep you doing what they want you to do: murder people." She leans in close to me. "They fucked with your head, Evans. And they're still fucking with your head."

"What are you saying?" I ask. "That they're not my dreams? That they're not memories?" I point at the television. "Are you saying she's not real? That she wasn't arrested last night?"

"She's an actress," Patrisse sighs.

"Change the channel," I shout, startling the others.

The gunman complies, and the television switches to additional coverage. The footage follows as she's processed and imprisoned in Trucast Tower. The holding cell is windowless and stark white. Trembling, the woman is helpless and scared. Two imposing staff members enter, decked out in full PPE gear. Next comes the strip search for all of America to see...

"Change it," I say, turning away.

The channel flips back to Milner and Candis, mid-interview. Candis clears her throat and reads a prepared question. "So why not detain Taylor's mother at a National Guard facility?" she asks. "Why here in Trucast Tower?"

Milner straightens. "Well, Candis," he starts. "This arrangement, made in conjunction with the Norton administration, was deemed the most probable for success."

Candis nods, then forces a smile. "I certainly appreciate all you do for the country," she says.

Milner studies Candis as if weighing the emotional trauma she has suffered. Sliding to the edge of his seat, he takes her hand in his.

"Look, Candis," he says. "I know this is hard on you and all of America. So, I want you to understand that what Evans has done, it's unacceptable. He's a terrorist, a traitor. And he never should've treated you this way."

Candis sobs as Milner pets her hand in an awkward sign of affection. "But Evans is an extreme menace and must be treated as such," Milner continues. "And that is why, if he does not turn himself over to authorities by twenty one-hundred hours tonight, his mother will be executed in his stead. Justice will be served; it must be served. Isn't that right, Candis?"

Candis nods, then smiles. "Justice will be served," she says, a little too happily.

"Either Evans turns himself in and faces punishment for all that he's done. Or she dies. The choice is his," Milner says.

"The choice is his," Candis says, practically breaking character altogether — she never was a good fake.

"Enough," I say, standing up. "Turn it off." The gunman shuts the television off and watches me wearily. "I need weapons, guns," I say, turning to Jackson. "I need transportation. I need…"

"Listen to me, Evans," Patrisse says, cutting me off. "This is how they get you back. This woman, she's the only memory you have because this is the only memory they gave you. If you were to go AWOL, they just parade her out. She's bait."

But for me, I keep staring at Jackson, our eyes locked. "I'm going for her, Jackson," I say. "I need weapons."

Patrisse sighs. "She is not your…"

"And what if you're wrong?" I snap, spinning toward her. "What if she is my mother, and I let her die? Then what?" I point at the television, its screen dark and inert. "That woman, she's the only hint of humanity that I have ever had. The only hope I had to cling to. If she dies…"

I trail off and look away. Jackson, he stands up and clears his throat. "I'm going with you," he says.

CHAPTER 21

Patrisse stares at Jackson as if he's insulted her. Janice and the masked gunmen, they watch uneasily. But Jackson holds his ground, gazing back at Patrisse, both patient and determined.

"This is it, Patrisse," he says. "This is why we've done everything that we've ever done. This is our chance."

Patrisse shakes her head, frustrated. She forces a laugh. "No," she says. "Not like this. This is foolish and stupid. They know you'll be coming. The cameras, the hammers, they'll all be waiting for you."

"It'll never be on our terms," Jackson says. "We've been sitting back, waiting for what? Years? It's been too long, Patrisse. Too many people have died. It's time to step up and do what we've prepared to do. If Evans wants to go, who better to follow?"

"You're going to get yourself killed," she says, her eyes darting between Jackson and me. "Both of you. Is that a part of your plan? And what about Jamal?" Patrisse snaps. "What's he going to do without you?"

Jackson looks at his boy. "Everything I do, I do for him, Patrisse. You know that," he says. "Since the day his mother was..." His eyes drift to the floor, pained by the memory of his wife's death. "Ever since we went on the run. Meeting you. Joining up with Dean and Janice." He gestures at Janice seated at the table, then at me. "Even you, Evans. Going down to the docks to meet you. That's all been for him. So he might have a future without living in fear."

"No," Patrisse says, shooting up out of her chair. She looks at Janice pleadingly. "Tell him, Janice. Tell him this is stupid. Tell him it's the last thing Dean would want. Not like this."

Janice shakes her head. "He knew Evans was a wild card," she says, glancing at me. "He changed everything."

"I won't let you do this," Patrisse says, growing more irate.

"I'm doing this with or without you, Patrisse," Jackson says.

"You're a fool, Jackson..."

As the back and forth continues, I glance between them, stunned by their discourse. Patrisse seems all too happy to put herself on the line, but not the people she cares about. I can't tell if that's selfish or selfless.

Me, I notice Jamal watching the exchange, wide-eyed. Quietly, I slide down to the floor, joining him on the blanket laid out on the cement. "What do you think, little man?" I ask him, my voice hushed.

"I think they want the same thing," he says critically. "They just don't know it."

I smile, impressed. "That's insightful," I say. "How'd you get to be so astute?"

Jamal shrugs. "My mom," he says.

I nod. Then lean toward him. "Mind telling me what happened to your mom?"

Jamal thinks, then looks at me. "She died," he says, matter of fact. "Shot. Killed. Something like that."

I blink. "Who shot her?" I ask, desperate to hide my anguish. Jamal keeps playing with his action figures. Carefully articulating their arms and legs, he makes them walk and jump. I watch him play before breaking the silence. "Was it me?" I ask, holding my breath.

Jamal sits there silent. Then he shakes his head. "No," he says, breaking a smile. "You're a good guy, Taylor Evans. Remember?"

Relief washes over me. I smirk, then smile. Jamal hands me my designated action figure. I take the toy, holding it proudly in my hand before realizing the others — Patrisse and Jackson, Janice, and the masked gunmen — have been watching me and the kid talk.

I stand up, looking from one to another.

"I'm going to save that woman, whether she's my mother or not. Because it's the right thing to do." I glance down at Jamal, and he nods back, encouraging me. "It will be dangerous. They will be ready. You're welcome to join. But I understand if you stay."

I let that sink in.

"Now," I say. "Weapons, transport. What can you offer me?" While the others look at me, unsure of what to say. Jackson smiles and nods. The nearest gunmen, the one with the limp, glances at the others wearily, then sighs.

"Ah, fuck it," he says. "If you need a ride, come this way." The gunman sets off through the garage with his cane, leading me around one car after another, each in various stages of repair or dismantling.

Patrisse shakes her head, exasperated. But she and the others follow. The gunman and I, we approach one vehicle singled out from the others. Hidden beneath a tarp, the gunman looks it over.

"I always knew this would come in handy," he says.

Pulling the tarp in one swoop, he reveals what lay beneath. From the flared fenders to its sweeping roofline, it's unmistakable: this is a hammermobile. But unlike the network's fleet, this one is patchwork and homemade — making it an even meaner-looking machine. No gloss or shine, all business.

"Holy shit," Jackson says, wide-eyed.

Me, I circle the car, running my fingers along its rough finish. "Where did you get this?" I ask.

The gunman snorts. "I made it," he says, proud.

I pause and look at the guy. "You made it?"

"Who do you think built yours?" he asks, reaching up for his mask. Pulling it off, he reveals his identity, and my jaw drops: it's Anton Williams, the network's lead mechanic — another turncoat.

This guy, he's been with the show as long as I have. These cars, the hammermobiles, they're his pride and joy. And that limp: I should've known it was him.

I think of our last interaction: I was strapped into the scramjet, about to launch on what would be my last mission with *The Eagle's Hammer*. Williams, he had limped up to me and bent down into my window.

"This car, it don't have to run in autonomous mode," he said. *"Have some fun with it."*

Staring at him now, I blink. I think of that night; I think of me dodging Blair's grenades. I was pinned against my hammermobile in the street, desperate. Then the car unlocked — but it shouldn't have, not after I defied my orders.

"Shit," I say. And here I thought it was Patrisse who had saved me, but this guy, he'd have access to the same programming...

Williams watches me, smug.

"It was you," I say. "You saved my ass that night, didn't you?"

Williams, he knows exactly what I'm talking about. He shrugs, then nods. "Guilty as charged," he says.

"Told you it wasn't me," Patrisse says, joining us.

The others follow behind her, circling the car. The other gunman steps forward, his gaze lingering on Williams. Then he turns to me.

"If you go in the front door," he says. "I'll get us in the back." He reaches up and pulls off his mask, revealing himself to be Zack, my long-time assistant. Again, my jaw drops. Three turncoats. But not just that, nobody was closer to me than Zack.

"Zack?" I ask, stunned. "Really?"

He looks at me, not with the eyes of some submissive personal assistant, but with the eyes of a man who knows what's at stake. He steps up next to Williams and takes his hand. I immediately get it, loud and clear. Everybody here, they're all doing this out of love. They're all doing this in the hope that maybe, just maybe, the future will be a better place.

Zack and me, we share a look of understanding. Then he turns to Patrisse. "We all have a lot to lose," Zack says, knocking his knuckles on the car's hood. "But if we want to make a difference in the world, this is it. This is our chance."

Patrisse says nothing. Her eyes shift from the two of them to Janice, then Jackson. "We can bring the network down," Jackson says. "Knock 'em off the air for good."

Patrisse looks at Janice. And though no words are spoken between them, Janice nods her approval. Patrisse, she swallows her pride and turns to me.

"I'll tell you what, Evans," she says. "I'll make you a deal. You save this woman. But you make the biggest show of it. I want the biggest spectacle this country has ever seen. All so nobody — not the nats, not the network, and certainly not the hammer — pay any attention to us. And I guarantee that we," she looks at the group, "we'll bring that fucking tower down."

She extends her hand and, locked in her gaze, I can't help but wonder if this — here in this garage somewhere in New Jersey — is this where the resistance dies?

Or is this where it truly begins?

Me, I think of the code word Patrisse shared with me back at the compound — the one that sent all the drones crashing into the hammers. My eyes narrow on her.

"You have another trick up your sleeve, don't you?" I ask.

Patrisse breaks a smile. "A big one," she says. I cock my head, waiting for more of an explanation. She giggles, then nods. "For years, I've been embedding a line of code deep into the scramjet's autonomous operating system. A line of code that'll make that little game with the hover-cams seem like child's play in comparison."

"The Eagle?" I ask, picturing the jet parked in its hanger, always fueled and always at the ready. Patrisse winks at me.

"It'll be one hell of a show," she says.

Janice steps next to Patrisse, wrapping an arm around her. "This is it," Janice says, looking at her and the others. "This is what we've worked so hard for. This is what Dean dreamed of: waking America up."

Janice squeezes Patrisse, urging her on.

Patrisse, she sets her jaw. "You want to take the network off the air?" she asks me. "Well, we're gonna take down the whole damn building."

I imagine it in my head. The jet streaking out of the sky, its collision with the building, the flames engulfing the tower. All of America watching as it collapses to the street below. The wreckage, the debris: it's a familiar iconography that the nation knows all too well. And Hanna Hernandez's just demise...

It's like a dream come true.

I smirk and nod. Patrisse smiles back at me, then extends her hand again. "We have a deal?" she asks.

I take her hand. And then we're packing. It's another fast-paced, quick-cutting montage with pounding bass and a sick guitar riff. You might think I'm back in the Eagle's Nest, gearing up with the other hammers, but no. I'm in New Jersey with a ragtag team of misfits... and I realize I love it.

Williams, he's amassed quite the collection of assault gear. Boots, fatigues, armor — it's all second or third hand, complete with the sweat stains and stench of the previous owners. But it's enough to make any slack-jawed Michigan militiaman proud.

Me, I'm looking in the mirror, and I like what I see. Patrisse, she tosses me a handgun and holster. I check the clip, slam it in place, and flash her a smile.

But all the up-tempo energy and comradery, it all comes to a screeching halt when I see the goodbyes. Williams and Zack, it's a long embrace. Because of his injury, they decided Williams should stay behind with Janice and the kid. But the mechanic, he's not happy about it. Zack, however, doesn't give him a choice. They hold each other, whispering into their ears.

Me, I'm about to slide into my custom-made hammermobile, all too aware that I've never felt love like that… that I've never received love like that. But I think of my mother, held captive in Trucast Tower. Maybe this is my chance…

There's a tug on my sleeve. It's Jamal, his father standing by his side. I kneel to the kid, and Jackson joins me. Jamal reaches into his fanny pack and pulls out our respective action figures, one for Jackson and me.

"Remember," Jamal says, handing them over. "You're the good guys."

Me, my heart just about breaks. "Thanks, kid," I manage to say. And I quickly enter the hammermobile, afraid to lose control of my emotions. Shutting the door, I adjust my rearview mirror — and that's when I see them: my victims.

From the backseat, they glare at me. And the kid's mother? She's here too. Dead, vengeful, and along for the ride.

"I love you, daddy," Jamal says, comforting his father.

Jackson nods, burying his head into his kid's shoulder, sobbing quietly.

Me, I fire up the hammermobile's motor. It's an old-school combustion engine, and it's like waking up a sleeping giant. I feel the beast rumbling through the steering wheel. As Williams limps toward the garage door, ready to open it. I glance at Patrisse…

Our eyes meet, and she stares back at me, silent. Finally, she nods. "Let's bust 'em," she says, and the dialogue sounds better coming from her than it ever did from me.

CHAPTER 22

You, you're watching as the network interrupts your regularly scheduled program. Three days you've been waiting, staring at your phone, eager for the notification. For three days, the country has been holding its breath, growing tense and uneasy.

The city, the nation, the world — everybody is on edge.

Three days ago, *The Eagle's Hammer* launched its assault on the compound, only to suffer a severe defeat. Desperate, the network paraded out my mother, much to the world's surprise — hammers aren't supposed to have histories, let alone mothers.

Over the last three days, you've watched the network try to act like nothing was out of the ordinary. On channel after channel, you watched the news anchors with their strained smiles and forced laughs. At work, around town, you watched as the collective anxiety grew.

You and your husband, your neighbors, nobody wanted to state the obvious for fear of retribution. But in your head, there's no denying it. Your entire life, the network has told you what to watch and what to think. It told you to live in fear and obey authority. But now, that authority is slipping through their fingers. Now, for the first time in your life: there is hope.

What happens next, nobody knows.

Me, I'm behind the wheel of Williams' homemade hammermobile. The expressway's unnaturally white LED streetlights flash by as I race toward the Walt Whitman Bridge. Beyond that, the city awaits my arrival. The expressway is empty, closed to traffic by orders of the National Guard — the road has been cleared for me and me alone.

With my hands clenching the steering wheel, my shoulder aches. But I stare ahead, eying the city's skyline with growing dread. I spot Trucast Tower, and a series of images flash in my mind: the hammers, Milner, Hernandez, and the woman, my mother…

My whole life is back there in the tower, right where I left it.

Along the side of the road, clumped between the streetlights, are curious onlookers. Dozens of them. Maybe hundreds. A week ago, these people would have been cowering in fear. Now they watch me with morbid curiosity, whispering to each other.

It's incredible the difference a few days can make.

The dash-mounted radio squawks. Williams has it conveniently tuned to the behind-the-scenes production frequency, allowing me to listen to the broadcast's communications. So far, the chatter has been sparse but thick with anticipation.

"We have visual confirmation," a staff member says, and a spotlight locks onto me, then another. I peak above and count a half-dozen hover-cams tracking my position.

Me drawing their attention, making my approach as clear as day; this is all part of our plan. The more eyes I draw, the less likely they'll notice Zack sneaking Patrisse and Jackson into the city. As far as the network knows, Zack is still just another happy Trucast employee. And with his security clearances and access codes, the three can walk in the back door.

Ahead of me, a row of armed personnel carriers spans the width of the suspension bridge, blocking all seven lanes. I slow to a crawl, unsure of what to expect: their plan could be just to trap me on the bridge. An airstrike would put an end to me in a flash. But that's not what the network wants — they want ratings.

Then, as I near, the center-most transport pulls ahead. The other vehicles follow suit, their movements, unnatural and alien as they are, create a V-shape similar to a flock of birds. Me, I nestle in behind them and match their speed. The transports then close in formation around me — this is my armed escort to Trucast Tower.

Looking them over, I see nothing past their mirror-finish windows, but I'm reminded of the first time I was led to the resistance's compound: the methodical march through the sewers that changed my life.

"Camera two," Riley says on the radio, the convoy and I approaching the far side of the river. "Hold your position and pan with the group as they pass. Ready camera two. And take."

I imagine what you, the viewer at home, must be seeing on the broadcast: the formation of vehicles crosses the river and exits the bridge. As we pass by, the camera pans and resolves on a spectacular establishing shot of the city.

Riley continues calling cameras like he's conducting a symphony, milking the drama for all it's worth. Me, I'm a little surprised how easy this is…

Then a set of headlights race up behind us.

Riley, his voice cracks. "What the hell?"

Eying my rearview mirror, I recognize the vehicle: it's a hammermobile — a real one. I look at the radio, intrigued. Clearly, this is off-script.

"CJ," Riley shouts. "What the hell are you doing?"

There's a drawn-out pause. Then CJ's voice blasts over the air. "He's killed three hammers," CJ says.

"Cut the bullshit," Riley says. "You should be back at the tower, awaiting further instruction," Riley scoffs. "I bet Riggs is with you too, isn't she?"

"Fuck off," Riggs answers.

"Typical," Riley laughs. "You're both fuckups. You know that? B-listers. Well, hold your position at the rear. We'll spin this like it was planned…"

"He's killed three hammers, Riley," CJ repeats. "And you're just going to let him waltz back like he owns the place."

"Bunch of bullshit," Riggs mumbles.

Riley lowers his voice. "Are you disobeying orders?" he asks. "Don't think you can't be replaced. Hell, we're replacing the whole team anyway. We might as well start clean…"

"Hey Riley," Riggs says. "I want you to take your orders and shove them up your ass." She howls with laughter. "Spin this," she says, and their radio cuts to static.

"CJ? Riggs?" Riley screams. "You're finished! You hear that? Done!" Riley turns to somebody in the control room. "Shut 'em down."

Me, I glance at the transports around me. We're approaching the exit for Broad Street, a narrow avenue compared to the expressway. From there, it's a straight shot north into the city.

Back in the control room, there's an uncomfortable silence. Then a production assistant chimes in. "The system's locked," she says, panicked.

"Locked?" Riley asks, clueless.

Me, I'm not surprised CJ is pissed. Riggs too. I *have* killed three hammers. That's unfathomable. I should've been killed on sight. But no, Hernandez and the network, they have to play this for ratings. They always do.

Realizing shit's about to go down, my eyes dart to my mirror. CJ drifts to the center of the road, flanking the nats and me. Riggs, she crawls out her window, gun in hand. She aims at the nearest transport… and opens fire.

You, you drop your bowl of popcorn. Your eyes, they're locked on the broadcast as Riggs' barrage of gunfire blows out the vehicle's front tire. The rim digs into the pavement, then buckles. The transport jerks violently and flips onto its roof. One down.

Me, I'm stuck in the middle of the formation with nowhere to go. CJ races up to fill the void, then smacks into my rear bumper. The steering wheel jerks in my hands, and I peer up at the mirror, catching a glimpse of CJ grinning at me.

The transports, their doors slide open, and teams of nats hang out, weapons at the ready. They aim and open fire. The bullets bounce off the hammermobile's armor plating. Then CJ cuts his wheel, swiping the right-most transport.

The vehicle is sent careening into a parked car, crashing violently. The other transports weave erratically. Bullets ricochet off my rear window as CJ and Riggs charge after me. I floor my accelerator, racing to within feet of the front-most transports. The vehicles clear a path for me, and I speed ahead.

CJ, he attempts to shoot the gap as well. But the two heavy transports close on him. Just as he's about to be smashed between them, CJ slams on his brakes. The transports collide. CJ swerves around the wreckage. Only two left.

The remaining transports shield me as I race ahead. I take the off-ramp, my tires screeching through the sharp right turn onto Broad Street. The vehicles and

CJ, they follow behind me, bouncing off each other like bumper cars.

Speeding along Broad Street, the area becomes more residential. Cars parked in the center of the avenue serve as dividers, separating the north and southbound lanes. Me, I dart over to the left lane as we cross an intersection. CJ and the transports are stuck to the right.

Overtop the cars, CJ and Riggs watch me pull ahead. Frustrated, Riggs reaches into the car and rummages around. Then, with a big smile, she reveals a rocket launcher. Before the lead transport can react, she takes aim and fires. The rocket streaks the short distance then connects...

KA-BOOM.

The explosion lights up the intersection, and the flaming wreckage flips end over end spectacularly. One transport left. CJ rams into the vehicle's rear end. The transport swerves, desperate. The nats take potshots as they pull alongside. But Riggs just laughs in their faces. She reloads the rocket launcher, takes aim, and pulls the trigger...

KA-BOOM.

The force of the explosion throws the transport into the parked cars, the twisted wreckage rolling over them. Now it's just them and me...

So, buckle up.

CHAPTER 23

Racing along Broad Street toward Center City, the buildings grow taller and taller. The divide between the two lanes ends, forcing us side by side, our hammermobiles a shadowy reflection of each other.

CJ sneers as Riggs loads another rocket. They inch closer. Sitting on the door frame, she levels the weapon over their vehicle's roof. I slam on my brakes as the rocket launches. It streaks in front of me, missing by mere inches before nailing a storefront.

KA-BOOM.

Glass and debris rain down, pelting the hood of my car. As Riggs watches the fireball climb into the sky, proud of herself, I yank my wheel toward them. Our fenders crunch together, and the impact jars the rocket launcher from her one hand, then the other. It clatters to the pavement; then it's gone.

Still hanging out the passenger window, Riggs glares at me, then flips me off.

Dead ahead of us now is city hall. The massive, ornate building sits at the city's center, and we turn onto Penn Square. Sliding around the corner, it's a quick jaunt before we're both cutting our wheels the other way, circling the building. We collide again, our fenders mangled and mashed as CJ tries pushing me into the curb. But these hammermobiles are beasts.

We slingshot down Rizzo Boulevard, side by side, racing toward Trucast Tower. Desperate, CJ slams into me. And then again. Both of us, our vehicles are pushing a hundred miles per hour when our fenders lock up.

Me, I fight the steering wheel to stay in control.

What happens next happens fast...

Both our vehicles hit the plaza's steps. We launch the stairs like a ramp, soaring into the air. The nose of my car shoots skyward, and the Eight-Four, way up at the top of the building, comes into view — and I know Hernandez is up there, watching the beautiful chaos below...

Still locked together, our vehicles rocket over the manicured bushes and decorative fountain of the building's plaza. We smash through the first set of lobby windows, then the second. Both cars smack off the floor, skipping like a rock on water. Airborne again, my vehicle twists atop theirs. Then we make landfall.

My windshield shatters, then implodes.

Me, I'm shielding myself from the heat and havoc.

The two vehicles, locked in a lover's embrace, begin to roll, crunching and crushing each other as they go. Then we're sliding on the marble, smashing through art sculptures, and demolishing benches until we finally crash into the bank of elevators along the far wall.

Upside down, I hang in my seat, barely conscious. I blink my eyes and feel my face. I'm a bloody mess but intact. I release the harness and collapse to the roof. Pain shoots from my shoulder, pulsating through my body, but I turn and look out the narrow opening that was my rear window.

The lobby is now a beautiful mess of destruction. But it's empty — no guards or nats.

Pulling myself out of the car, I hear a whimpering from the other wreckage. "Somebody help," CJ says, his voice echoing in the cavernous space. "Would somebody please come fucking help me?"

Me, I climb to my feet, and my boots crunch on broken glass as I approach him.

"Ah, fuck," he says, spotting me. He desperately lunges toward his weapon, but it's just out of reach. With a mangled leg pinned beneath his seat, it's a lost cause.

I crouch down near him, then pick up the handgun for myself. Peering into the wreckage, I spot Riggs. Still strapped into her harness, hanging upside down, she's out cold. A nasty gash across her forehead makes me think she smacked her head off the car's roof pillar.

"Evans," CJ says, still struggling to free himself. "Help me, man. Get me out of here." I stand up and look at him — what a pathetic sight. "Look," CJ says, gesturing about the lobby. "There's nobody here, man. No cameras. It's just you and me."

I motion toward Riggs. "And her," I say.

CJ rolls his eyes. "Kill her," he says. "Shoot her while she's out cold."

"And what of you?" I ask, leveling the gun at him.

He clenches his eyes shut, terrified. "Come on, Evans," he says. "We're a team, man. You and me. Let me go, let me out of here, and I won't tell anybody. They'll think you left me for dead. Come on…"

"Mercy?" I ask. "You're asking for mercy? Hammers don't grant mercy, CJ. You know that." I chamber a round, savoring the CHA-CHK sound it makes.

CJ flinches. Over in the passenger seat, Riggs' eyes flutter in an attempt to open.

"Fuck that," CJ says, frustrated that it's me standing over him. "Nobody's here, Evans. Nobody's watching."

"Back at the resistance, would you have granted me mercy?" I ask.

CJ blinks. We both know the answer to that one. "That was the show, man," he says.

Over in her seat, Riggs mumbles incoherently. Her hands feel about, fumbling with her harness. I gesture toward her. "She's coming to," I say.

"Get me out of here, and I'll kill her myself," he says, determined.

I nod — what a piece of shit. For a moment, I stop and think of Zack and Williams' goodbye that I had witnessed before leaving the garage. True love is so easy to recognize. Then I focus on CJ. I'm betting a man like this has never loved anybody other than himself… though the same could be said about me, I suppose.

"You're pathetic," I say.

Then I toss the gun at Riggs. Hitting her in the chest, she startles awake. She glances about, groggy and confused. Blinking and squinting, she focuses her eyes on the handgun now within reach.

She looks at CJ, then at me.

I smile back at her.

"You son of a bitch," CJ says, now clawing back into the vehicle, again stretching for the weapon. But Riggs, she knows what's happening now too. She reaches for the gun. But it's also just out of her reach. Desperate, she fumbles at her harness's release...

It's a race.

"Good luck, you two," I say, standing and walking toward the elevators. As I approach, the doors slide open, and I step inside. I press the button for the studio training facility, and as the elevator doors slide shut, a gunshot rings out...

BAM.

CHAPTER 24

While you were watching me approach those armored
personnel carriers back on the Walt Whitman Bridge, what
you didn't see was Zack sneaking into the city with Patrisse
and Jackson hiding in his trunk.

You didn't see the network security guards, their eyes
glued to their mobile devices, wave Zack into the below-
parking deck, oblivious to how odd his arrival was at this
time of night. You didn't see the empty corridors and
unattended elevators that greeted them inside. And you
didn't see Zack swiping his employee badge over and over,
granting them access deeper and deeper into the building.

While you watched CJ and I race toward the tower,
you didn't see the elevator carrying them to the studio floor.

You didn't hear the elevator chime before the doors slid open. And you didn't see the guards glance briefly at Zack, oblivious to Patrisse and Jackson tucked to the sides.

No, you didn't see any of that. Nobody did. It wasn't until Jackson pressed the cold, steel tip of his carbine to that security guard's temple that anybody — anybody at all — knew something was wrong. Just like Pearl Harbor, or 9/11, or D.C., by the time people realized what was happening: it was already too late.

You, at home in your living room watching with your family, you don't see the crew's stunned flushed-with-fear faces as Zack bursts into the control room, gun in hand. And you don't see the panic-stricken reactions of the news anchors and pundits as Patrisse and Jackson charge into the studio, their assault rifles at the ready.

In the control room, Riley leaps out of his seat. He grabs an assistant, shielding himself as Zack approaches.

"Nobody move," Zack shouts, training his gun from one staff member to the next. They stare at him, arms raised. Zack steps up to the technical director and reaches over her. On the production switcher, he presses the button for the studio camera.

You at home, you're enthralled. But instead of watching CJ and I launch our hammermobiles into the building's lobby, the broadcast cuts unexpectedly to the studio.

On-screen, Skylar and Silas have their hands raised. They're looking off-camera, scared shitless.

Patrisse, she steps up to the anchor desk.

"What the hell do you think you're doing?" Silas asks, aware of his tally light and desperate to seem tough. Patrisse, her gun trained on him, motions for him to move.

"Get up," she says. "Let's go."

"Fuck off," Silas says, his teeth clenched. "This is my desk."

Patrisse sighs. She smacks him with the butt of her gun, and he collapses to the floor. Staff members cry out, scared. Skylar stares down at him, shocked.

"Bitch," Patrisse says, snapping her fingers in front of Skylar's face. "Leave." Skylar is up and out of her chair without hesitation, abandoning Silas as he struggles to stand. "Here," Patrisse says, reaching for him. "Let me help."

She grabs a handful of hair and drags him off set, screaming. As he's about to flee, Jackson grabs him by the collar and shoves him into the camera.

"Frame up the shot," Jackson says.

You, you can't believe your eyes. You watch as Patrisse sits down at the desk and collects herself. Looking into the camera, she stares right into the heart and soul of everyone watching.

"America," Patrisse says. "We need to talk…"

You and your husband, you slide to the edge of your couch. Your kid, watching from the floor, he backs up to your knees, and you put an arm around him, holding him.

None of you dares blink.

"This is not who we are. And this is not who we want to be," Patrisse says. She gestures about the studio. "This America — the America they're selling you — it's a fraud. For too long, we've let ourselves be misled. For too long, we've trusted the wrong people. The wealthy. The one percent. They happily handed over the keys of our kingdom. They nurtured this corporatocracy, and it's they who ushered in this era of terror. The elite, they shut their eyes to these atrocities while we — you and I — we had to watch them, we had to endure them. And their reasons were simple. Greed. Money. Power. This system of control, perverted as it is, it benefited them and them alone. It increased their wealth at our expense.

"Look around. Look at each other. Look at our nation and ask: what happened? Is this who we have always been? Hate-filled, back-stabbing, and callous? Have we always fed off the pain and humiliation of each other? Or is this who they want us to be? Is this how they've trained us to be?

"Divided, we are weak. When separated and tribal, we can be controlled. What emotions do we feel anymore but fear and rage? Fear of them. But rage at each other. Well, it's time we wake up, America. We are not each other's enemies. It's them." Patrisse points upward, off-camera. "It's the oligarchs behind the scenes, pulling the strings.

"So, how do we fix this? We do it together. They are weak and few, hiding behind wealth," she says, pointing upward. "Together, we are strong. Together, we can punch up, not down. Not at each other. So here I am now, in front of you, my fellow Americans. And I'm asking you now to resist. Together, we can change all this. We can put an end to this terror today. By building strong communities, forged of hope and compassion, not hate and fear, we can do this."

Patrisse pauses, then nods. "Yeah, it's scary," she continues. "What I'm asking from you is not a little. It's a lot. But we need more than light right now; we need fire. We need more than a gentle rain shower; we need thunder. Yes, it may be a dangerous path forward. But the alternative…"

She motions around the studio. "You know the alternative. The terror. The bloodshed. How many loved ones have you lost? How many loved ones will you lose? It's more than racial injustice or income inequality. It's more than just the National Guard or *The Eagle's Hammer*. It's those that pull their strings, this network included. They're dealers of fear. They deliver it to you nightly. And it's your terror they accept as payment. They want you to live in fear. Of them, yeah. But more so of each other. And of ourselves.

"But you already knew this, didn't you?" she asks. "You've already thought this. Secretly. Sometimes ashamed. The idea of freedom and liberty. Of basic human rights. These ideas have been so restricted they're practically illegal. But the limits of their tyranny..." she points upward again. "Are only determined by the acceptance of the oppressed."

Patrisse lowers her finger toward the camera. She points right at the lens. "You," she says. "Have you had enough?"

You, in your living room, the television flickering before you, you've never seen anything like this before. You, your husband, your kid — you've been listening with an intensity you didn't even know you had. It's been like Patrisse was speaking directly to you. As if she knew the fear and shame you've felt. As if she knew all the hopeless tears you've cried.

And now, she's telling you that you can do something. You take your husband's hand, and he squeezes yours...

Hope. You feel hope.

"This is America," Patrisse says, nodding. "But what makes this nation so remarkable, so divine, is its ability to change. Who will step up to lead this charge? Who takes the reins of the people, for the people? I have no idea. But I know we will find the right people when we need them.

For its movements that make leaders, not leaders that make movements."

Me, I've been watching all of this too. Riding the elevator up, my attention has been locked on the video screen mounted in the corner. Me, I've been watching Patrisse: the way her eyes sparkle, the way her mouth moves. And I've been listening to the ideas she is planting in our heads — yours, mine, America's.

Me, I'm on my way to Milner. To save my mother and settle my debts once and for all. But that last line rings in my ears…

Movements make leaders.

CHAPTER 25

The elevator chimes, and the doors open. I pull my handgun, chamber a round, and peek out into the hall. It's empty. Stepping out, the entrance to the locker room is to my left. But to my right, the corridor turns to the training facility. Keeping my back along the wall, I enter the studio expanse and find Milner exactly where I expected to...

A good hammer always knows their way home.

Milner stands in the middle of the facility, gun in hand. Next to him, bound and gagged, is the woman... my mother. They're surrounded by studio cameras, a large jib, and other broadcast equipment but no crew or staff. It looks like the network was planning on making quite the show out of this encounter — but I crashed the party early.

"Let her go," I say, stepping into the light.

Milner, he sneers. "Now, that's no way to greet your mother," he says. He looks at the woman, then, with mock compassion, he fixes her hair and adjusts the gag. Struggling against the restraints, she's terrified and exhausted. "You've been a bad boy, Evans," he says. "Didn't anybody tell you not to go around killing hammers?"

I slowly approach them, my gun still raised. Nearing, my eyes dart toward the woman, lingering on her the closer I get — I can't deny our similarities. Her eyes, her chin; they're all mine.

"Don't remember her, do you?" Milner asks, amused by my curiosity. "Your dear old mother?"

The comment stirs more emotion out of the woman. Her bloodshot eyes meet mine, and she tries to speak — but the gag makes it impossible. She chokes and heaves as tears run down her cheeks.

"I'm here," I say to Milner. "You got me. Now, let her go."

Milner shakes his head, then waves his gun in my direction. "Good line, Evans," he says. "Well delivered. Heroic and brave. But this," he gestures about the facility, at the dormant cameras and equipment. "This is off-script now. This is between you and me. One final lesson before the big finale."

My eyes narrow. "Stop playing games," I say.

Milner snorts. "I don't care about the politics of all this," he says. "And neither should you. The hammer. The network. It's beneath people like you and me." He walks around the woman, circling her. "This woman, she means nothing. Whether she's your mother or not, she means nothing. The sooner you learn that, the better. This empathy you've acquired, this compassion. It's toxic. And it will consume you, weaken you. Emotions dull the blade, son. Don't let that happen to you."

I take another few steps closer, prompting Milner to level his weapon. But not at me, at her.

"Don't hurt her," I say, stopping. "Let her go."

Milner hesitates as if to consider it. Then he places the gun to her head. The woman coils away, sobbing uncontrollably. Milner, he loves it. The sadistic son of a bitch is pure masochistic evil. And, more than ever, I recognize the shadowy reflection he is of me. Celebrated hammer. American hero. But I've chosen a far different path...

I back away, a palm raised in retreat.

Milner looks between the two of us, then raises an eyebrow. "Is there anything you wish to say to her?" he asks. "Anything you want to ask?" He yanks the gag out of her mouth. She gasps for air. "Go ahead," he says. "Talk."

I blink. The woman gazes at me, her lips trembling. I think of her in my dreams. I think of her comforting and soothing me, night after night. Are they memories? Or implants? Were they triggered emotions to help me cope with the horror I witnessed daily? The atrocities I was complicit in? Was she simply a tool for keeping me in check? Or is she real?

Now, the first thing I think to say is what she would always say to me. "Everything's going to be okay," I say. "I promise."

Milner huffs. "Now, don't be a pussy, Evans," he snaps. "Ask her."

I shake my head. The answer, it doesn't even matter.

"Fine," Milner barks. "I'll ask her for you." He turns to the woman, then grabs her chin. "Are you his mother? Go ahead and tell him."

Me, I hold my breath. The woman, she glances between us, sobbing harder. Finally, she answers. "Yes," she whimpers.

Milner laughs, then quickly stuffs the gag back into her mouth. "There it is," he says.

But the woman, the way her eyes linger on Milner... I can't help but question her sincerity. Is she telling me yes because she is my mother? Or because they're forcing her to say yes?

I think of Hernandez and all the ways she has to force people to do what she wants. They go far beyond paychecks and tend to involve hostages. If your life doesn't mean shit to yourself, certainly there's somebody else's that does. And Hernandez will find them.

Is that the case today? I shake the doubt out of my head. It doesn't matter, I tell myself. Save the woman.

"I'm here, Milner," I say. "I don't care if she's my mother or not. She's bait, okay? Well, you got me. Let her go." I bend over, place my gun on the polished floor, and kick it toward him — immediately regretting the decision.

Even Milner stares at me, stunned.

Me, I raise my hands above my head and step forward.

"You got me. Do what you want with me." I look around us, at the dark void surrounding us. "I'm here," I shout, assuming Hernandez must be watching — she always is. "Hang me! Shoot me! Just let her go!"

I listen to my voice echo off the walls, then fall silent. I wait for a response. I wait for the lights to fade up to reveal a couple dozen nats, armed and ready. I wait for Hernandez to step forward, clapping her satisfaction. "Bravo," she might say. "Well done."

But none of that happens. All I hear are the woman's labored breaths. And then I see them: my victims. In the dark, their eyes glistening and expectant. They've found me. Or I've found them…

Milner frowns with genuine disappointment. Then, setting his jaw, he levels his gun at me. I step toward him — maybe this is what I want: to have my life end here in the training facility, at the hands of Milner. It might not be the death by hanging I've long fantasized about; I won't be answering for the network's crimes against humanity, but my victims: they'll gladly take care of me from here.

But this woman: will the network let her go? Probably not. Not if she's my mother. But once that trigger is pulled, it won't be my problem. Not anymore. This is for the best, I tell myself. My throng of victims, I know they're waiting to have their way with me. In hell, or wherever, they are primed and ready to have their revenge…

Jamal's mother included.

"Go ahead," I say. "Finish me."

"You're sick, Evans," Milner says. "Your mind, it's all twisted up. That's why I'm doing this for you. To set you free of this burden. This is for your own good."

Milner's finger begins to squeeze the trigger, and I close my eyes, thankful. I picture my victims surrounding me, ready to catch my soul before my body even hits the floor. They are hungry, and it is time…

BAM.

Feeling a mist of blood on my face, I open my eyes and see the woman, my mother, tipping over. She falls to the ground, a gaping entry wound in her skull. Milner, he's not looking at her — he's looking at me, wide-eyed and eager.

He killed her, not me. My eyes meet his, furious. Why would he do this? Because he is evil; because he is the proto-hammer of which we are all sliced. Forged in a society steeped in division and radicalization in which everything — even this woman's life — is a zero-sum game.

Milner, standing before me, savoring my anguish, is everything perverted and wrong with this nation, with our humanity. And it's time to put an end to it all…

I slap the gun out of the old man's hands. I hit it so fast, so hard, that he never even sees it coming. The piece clanks on the studio floor and slides into the darkness. And that's when I see Milner's first hint of fear. I've seen this look a thousand times, in countless faces. Milner is right about one thing: blood is addictive. When it hits your system, it's like a drug.

And now, our victims are coming out of the void, both Milner and mine…

But I find I am no longer afraid of them. The fear they would bring, it's no longer here. It's like they're no longer here for me, but here with me. I realize they want blood, his blood. The thousands of dead, they're here to enjoy the show...

Spectacle, I think. Give them spectacle.

Milner knows his time has come. He pulls a knife because that's what he was trained to do. If your primary weapon fails you, resort to your secondary. But it won't matter. Just like the hundreds of victims he killed — Jamal's mother included — in this fleeting last moment of his life, he thinks there's a chance...

His victims, they begged because that's all they could do. Milner, he shoves the knife into my abdomen because that's all he can do. But it won't change the inevitable. The blade slices through my flesh into muscle. The pain is searing and intense, but I do not care, not now...

Because I am Taylor Evans; I am The Eagle's Hammer.

I grab his wrist, the blade still in my flesh and twist. I twist until the old man's cartilage tears and his ligaments pop. I hear it; he feels it. I watch his pupils dilate. His panic hits like clockwork, a chemical reaction that not even his years of dedicated training can prevent. I slap him across the face, demoralizing him. The blow stings. He staggers away from me, clutching his wrist.

Leaving the knife in my side, I lunge at him. I grab his throat with both hands and pull him close. He collapses, and I follow him to the floor. Now atop of him, I hesitate

— as if to let the cameras reposition themselves and set their shots.

I wait for a beat, then lean in close to him…

This is it, the big moment.

Now's the time for me to deliver a perfect line of dialogue encapsulating our whole story arc, a poignant one-liner that bookends this mentor-apprentice relationship…

Milner, he watches me expectantly. The showman in him can't help but be enthralled by my performance. But instead of saying something iconic, instead of saying something to be quoted and repeated in popular culture for years to come, all I say is: "St. Louis."

On cue, the massive LED panels emerge from the darkness and begin to configure themselves into the city's streets. Milner — and his head, in particular — is just outside the safety zone. It's now that he realizes I have him pinned down in the path of a panel. The showman can't help but smile. *Now, that's spectacle…*

A panel swoops toward us, smashing into his face. His nose breaks, and his teeth shatter. The panel wobbles, then falls. The city of St. Louis flickers onto the screens around us.

Me, I heave Milner up, then slam him down along another track. "Chicago," I say.

Again, the LED panels are on the move, sliding and twisting as they reconfigure. And again, Milner is pinned in their path... WHACK.

The blow snaps his neck at an angle that I know is bad, real bad. But I'm not done yet.

"Trenton," I say, throwing the still moving panels into disarray. Running into each other, they begin to tip and fall, dominoing around us and shattering against the floor. It's mayhem. But I slide Milner through the woman's blood — my mother's blood — into the path of yet another panel...WHACK.

I feel him go limp. I feel the life slip out of him. But I don't stop there, not with his victims present. With them cheering me on, I name all the cities he terrorized. All the communities that lived in fear of him, and me — and of *The Eagle's Hammer*. The poor and oppressed communities that society abandoned long ago...

By the time I'm done, his head is barely attached to his body. Blood is everywhere, both his and my mother's, mixing. I stand up and look at my work — no need for a trial or a public hanging. What's done is done.

This, this is my masterpiece; Milner would be proud. Like he always said...

Blood is good for ratings.

CHAPTER 26

"Now go," Jackson shouts, his rifle in hand. "Get the hell out of here!" The terrified production crew pours out of the studio and into the hall. Riley and the staff exit the control room, joining the others as they head toward the elevators and stairwells.

Me, I'm walking upstream, bumping into panicked staff members as they run for their lives. Upon recognizing me, their hysterics leap to a whole other level. Here I am: the murderer returned. And with Milner's blood still on my hands, I don't fault their terror.

Riley, he spots me and hesitates. With his back against the far wall of the hall, he's unsure if he should risk approaching me. For a moment, as other employees scurry past, he seems about to say something to me. An insult, perhaps? I have, after all, really fucked up his television show. But Riley clamps up and races by.

Silas and Skylar, they spot me as well. But besides Silas's disdain, they keep moving.

So much for reunions.

Pushing through the studio door, I find Jackson at the news desk, the studio now empty except for him. From the look on his face, he knows what I've done.

"I'm sorry about your mother," he says.

I nod. "I'm sorry about Jamal's mother," I say.

Jackson hesitates, then nods. "Come on. Let's go," he says.

He leads me into the production booth. Patrisse sits at a computer terminal, typing out long lines of code. Zack, he hovers over her, on guard.

As Jackson and I approach, I point out a row of security camera-feeds on the monitor wall. Nats are pouring into the building, swarming around the wrecked hammermobiles in the lobby. Some greet the fleeing production staff — Riley and Silas in particular — as they dump out of the elevators.

"We don't have much time," I say.

"Almost done," Patrisse snaps.

Her fingers are a blur as she types at a dizzying speed. Me, I try to follow along. The interface is that of the Eagle's autonomous flight deck. I manage to make out the word 'destination' to which she quickly adds this building's address here in Center City. Several FAA flight restrictions pop up, but she overrides them with ease.

Next, she's prompted for the launch time. She answers 'immediate.' Then, with finality, she hits the enter button, executing the command. Patrisse stares at the screen, stunned that she's finally done it. With that keystroke, she's achieved what Dean and Janice had only dreamt of accomplishing: the network's demise.

A countdown clock pops up. Patrisse stands and gestures toward the terminal. "There it is," she says. "Fifteen minutes and counting."

Zack looks over her shoulder and gushes. "That was easy," he says.

The four of us stand there staring at the countdown, watching the numbers twirl by. It's mesmerizing. Though the actual flight will take only minutes, prepping the jet, taxiing to the runway, and clearing the airspace will chew up some time. The process is fully automated, though. In fact, there probably isn't a single human on-site to abort the jet's suicide mission.

Me, I imagine the hangar's massive doors sliding open. I picture the scramjet taxiing itself onto the tarmac. I hear the engines begin their pre-flight check sequence. In fifteen minutes, the Eagle will be screaming toward this tower at around Mach 6 — like a bat out of hell.

"We gotta get out of here," Patrisse says, snapping me from my daze. She swings her rifle at the computer terminal. Then, with the butt of the weapon, she smashes the machine.

"Let's move," Jackson says, heading for the door. He checks the hallway — all clear, for now. We hurry out.

The hallway is quiet and ominous, especially knowing what destruction awaits it. We blow past the elevators and continue toward the north-end emergency stairwell. But as we round the corner, the door opens, and I catch a flash of blue —it's the nats, and a lot of them.

Dammit, they're already here. Me, I grab Jackson and Patrisse by their collars, pulling them back around the corner. The nats open fire, tagging Zack as he tries to leap to safety. He drops to the floor, screaming in pain.

"Zack!" Patrisse shouts. She reaches for him, but it's futile; gunfire keeps her at bay.

Rolling onto his back, Zack glares at his assailants. He chambers a round and opens fire, blasting a handful of them. They collapse in the doorway. But their backups, now shielding themselves behind their fallen comrades, take aim and fire.

Zack is brutalized, the bullets thudding into his now lifeless body. Me, I think of Williams. I think of their final goodbye. I think of all the targets who never saw their loved ones again.

The gun smoke triggers the fire suppression system. The alarm sounds, and recessed sprinklers turn on, showering the hall with water.

Patrisse cries out, then staggers back. I grab her carbine and take a few potshots around the corner with Jackson. It's enough to keep them at bay for now.

"We won't hold them for long," Jackson shouts. Wiping water off his face, he glances down the corridor toward the other stairwell. "And if they flank us, we're finished."

Patrisse eyes me. "The elevators?" she asks.

I consider, then nod. I know you've heard it before: when no options are good options, go with the least bad option. Today, those elevators, death traps that they may be — that's our least bad option.

"Let's go," I say. Ditching our position, we sprint to the elevators, slipping on the wet floor. Patrisse slides up first and presses the down button. The center elevator opens as if it'd been waiting for us.

"This isn't right," Patrisse says, backing away wearily.

"What are you talking about?" Jackson asks, frantic.

He steps toward the elevator, but Patrisse grabs his arm.

"It's a trap," she says, holding him back.

Me, I spot the nats rounding the corner. I flip over a couch and pull Patrisse down just as the team opens fire. The furniture is shredded. Bullets pound the tile. The lights above us, they shatter and burst. Then all we see are the cool-blue muzzle flashes as the nats come at us like a zombie army. Nameless, faceless, and never-ending.

I fire blindly over the furniture. Jackson, he's got eyes on the other side of the hallway. When he spots the first nat turning the other corner, he jumps to his feet.

"Time's up," he says, grabbing Patrisse and me. With brute strength, he throws us into the elevator… exposing himself to the onslaught. Bullets riddle his body. Patrisse and I, we smack into the far side of the car as Jackson stumbles in behind us.

"Jackson!" Patrisse shouts, realizing his injuries.

Ignoring her, Jackson smacks the button that closes the door. As they shut, I catch a glimpse of approaching nats. They open fire, pockmarking the now-closed doors from the hallway. In between floors, Jackson mashes the emergency-stop button and the elevator jerks to a halt.

Satisfied, he collapses into me. Together, we slide to the floor. Cradling him in my legs and holding him in my arms, his blood soaks my clothing.

"Hang in there, Jackson," Patrisse says, kneeling over him. "We're going to get you help."

Jackson snorts. He looks at me above him. "Evans," he says. "I got something for you." He reaches into his pocket, grimacing in pain. He pulls out his action figure. "Take this," he says, placing it in my hand. "Make sure it gets back to my boy." He closes my fingers around it. "He could use a friend now, alright?"

Not sure what to say, I nod.

Jackson smiles at me, his teeth soaked with blood.

"Jackson, no," Patrisse says, sobbing.

But Jackson takes his last breath; then he's gone. Me, I look at the toy, turning it in my fingers. This action figure, it looks nothing like him. Not that any of them do. But this one seems particularly fitting for the man now dead in my lap. Despite its faded paint and exposed plastic, there's no doubting this figure is a hero. You know the moment you see it — just like Jackson.

A good guy... till the very end.

"Goodbye, friend," I say to Jackson, carefully sliding out from beneath him. I set his head down gently on the floor, then slip the action figure into the same pocket as mine. This man was everything I wanted to be, whether I realized it or not. And now he's dead...

"We have to go," Patrisse says. "We're running out of time." Wiping the tears from her cheeks, she releases the emergency-stop and presses the button for the basement. But nothing happens. Then she presses the button for the lobby. Nothing. "What the hell?" Patrisse asks, now smashing buttons at random.

"This elevator's only going to one floor," I say without looking at her. "The Eight-Four."

Patrisse hesitates. She looks at that button on the panel, then shakes her head. "No, Evans," she says. "Let's get the hell out of here."

"I have to finish this," I say. "Hanna Hernandez. On the Eight-Four. She's the one behind all of this. The network. The hammer. Her time has come."

Patrisse looks me over, then shakes her head. "When that scramjet hits this building, she'll be the first to die, Evans. And we won't be far behind her if we don't get out of here." She looks above us, studying the elevator. "I have an idea," she says. Taking the tip of her rifle, she jabs at the elevator's ceiling. An access panel pops open. Patrisse's eyes light up. "We climb out of this. There's got to be a main-tenance ladder or something along the shaft." She widens her stance and crouches down. "Lift me up there, and I'll check it out."

Me, I don't move a muscle. "I'm a hammer," I say. "Hammering is what I do. It's what I'll die doing."

Patrisse stares at me, her mind spinning the possibilities. She's thinking of what to say — the right thing to say. For once, I don't mind the silence. Instead, I look deep into those beautiful eyes — I could stare into them all day. Finally, Patrisse steps toward me.

"Don't leave me, Taylor," she says, sliding her hand into mine. "I've lost everything. I don't want to lose you too."

The use of my first name, the tone of her voice, her intimate touch — this takes me by surprise. She leans against me, and I'm reminded of my mother: not the woman dead in the training facility, but the woman in my dreams. Those feelings of comfort and security, they wash over me.

Patrisse glances at my lips, then dives for them. Stunned, we kiss, but my confusion quickly melts away as I embrace her. My head floods with glimpses of potential futures: I picture her naked in my arms. I imagine her laughing at a joke. I think of us together, facing this uncertain future... but we're together. And I like that.

On the video screen mounted in the corner, the network feed cuts away from the abandoned anchor desk in the studio. Patrisse and I, embracing each other, we don't see it. But when a familiar voice begins to speak, it doesn't take long for us to recognize it...

"Help me, Evans. Please help me."

Patrisse and I pull apart and look at the monitor. It's Jamal, his eyes swollen and bloodshot from crying. His surroundings, I place them immediately: Hernandez's office.

"No," I shout, lunging helplessly at the screen.

Patrisse holds me back. But she, too, is startled.

The image of Jamal zooms out to a wide shot that includes Hernandez herself, looming over the kid. She caresses his head, running her fingers through his hair. She looks up at the camera, at me. And smiles.

"You weren't really going to leave without saying goodbye, were you?"

CHAPTER 27

Patrisse presses the button for the Eight-Four, and the elevator begins its long ascent.

"Evans," she says, looking me over. "Listen to me. When we get up there, Hernandez, the network, they're going to trick you. They're going to pull whichever little string will bring you back. Whatever they say, whatever they do: it's bullshit. Your whole life, they've been pulling your strings like a puppet. Cut the strings. Don't listen to them, not anymore."

Me, I avoid her gaze. There's so much going through my head right now that I'm struggling to focus. But in a matter of moments, I'll be standing face to face with the most dangerous individual in the country: Hanna Hernandez.

So, I better get my game face on.

"Listen to me, Evans," Patrisse says, demanding my attention. "They're gaslighting you. This is how they do it. They twist the truth until it's unrecognizable. They tell so many lies that you no longer recognize the truth when it's right in front of you. This is how they'll get you back. They'll confuse and frustrate you until this..." Stepping forward, she points to my head. "This stops working. Then you'll do whatever they want. They'll be in control, whether you realize it or not."

I turn from her, checking what ammunition we have left.

Frustrated, Patrisse grabs my shoulders and gets in my face. "Look at me. Be strong. We can do this," she says.

"Do I not look strong to you?" I snap. Pulling away from her, I search for my reflection in the elevator's polished brass accents. Finding myself, I stand up straight and tall. "I'm Taylor Evans, American hero."

"You look broken, Evans," she says with blunt honesty. "You look shattered. You have for years. That's how we knew you'd turn."

I blink. Considering what she said, I look at my reflection again. And maybe she's right. I'm ragged and unkempt.

I haven't shaved in days — hell, I haven't showered in days. I'm pale and exhausted. Disgusted with myself, I close my eyes and look away. But behind my eyelids, I picture, of all things, the action figure Jamal had given me. Its paint faded and worn... just like me.

I'm one of the good guys.

Patrisse steps up next to me. She places her palm on my cheek, then gently turns my head toward her. "Together," she says softly. "That's how we got here. And that's how we finish this. We rescue Jamal. We kill Hernandez. We destroy the network. And we do it together."

We stare at each other, eyes locked. Finally, I nod.

"Let's bust 'em," I whisper — delivering my catchphrase for what I hope is the last time.

The elevator slows and chimes. We level our weapons, ready for anything. A team of nats could be waiting for us. But when the bullet-riddled doors slide open, we find nothing. The waiting area just outside the elevator is empty, but, as always, I think of Joaquin Rogers, the director Hernandez had personally filleted here in front of the entire production crew...

How would he have directed these scenes?

What story would he be telling?

Patrisse and I, we hear the bustling sounds of Jamal playing. It's faint, but it draws us out of the elevator and toward the entrance to Hernandez's office. Cautiously, we step into the doorway and find Jamal and Hernandez at her desk, the two duking it out with the kid's action figures.

Hernandez spots us and greets us with a smile.

"Oh, hello there," she says. Jamal looks up at us, uncertain and scared. He's been crying. But the kid, bless his heart, is as brave as his father. "Come join us," Hernandez says. "But please, leave the weapons at the door."

Patrisse and me, we glance at each other. Neither of us is sure if we should give in.

Hernandez eyes us with a playful smirk. "I insist," she says, flashing a handgun she's been holding behind her back — a threat directed at Jamal.

We carefully set our weapons on the floor, then enter. As we pass through the doorway, I spot somebody sitting at the furniture arrangement near the window. The figure is hunched over and sobbing.

"I don't think any introductions are necessary here," Hernandez says. "We're all old friends, aren't we?" The person seated on the couch, they turn slowly toward us, wiping tears from their cheeks: it's Janice.

"I'm sorry," Janice says. "So sorry."

Patrisse and I are puzzled. Then glancing between Janice and Hernandez, Patrisse pieces it together.

"How could you?" Patrisse snaps. "How could you do this?"

Janice sobs. "I'm so sorry," she mutters.

"Janice," Hernandez says. "Why don't you join us here at the adult table." She looks at Patrisse and me. "Come and sit, all of you," she says.

We again obey her — she's got the gun after all. And I can see how much she enjoys wielding it. A simple weapon like that, she rarely gets to use them herself. But the situation we have here, this is special. And she's undoubtedly savoring it — again, the image of Joaquin bleeding out on the floor comes to mind. That situation was special too. And I remember Hernandez standing over him, knife in hand. You'd have thought it was the best sex of her life.

As I slide into the chair, Hernandez eyes me. "Janice here tells me you've had quite the adventure." She gestures toward my shoulder. "And a quick recovery." — me, I think of the synthetic polymer they had applied to the entry wound, the antibiotics used to treat my infection. Is that how we had access to such high-end medical supplies?

I glance at Patrisse, perplexed. But she's glaring at Janice. "What were you thinking?" Patrisse asks.

Janice shrugs. "I just thought: what if we started working with them instead of against them? Maybe we'd make progress? Maybe we'd…" She trails off as whatever justification she had, its logic fades when spoken.

"Dean," Patrisse says. "He's dead because of you. Jackson and Zack, they're dead now too, Janice." Patrisse watches her begin to tremble, then sob. She motions toward Jamal, his action figures still splayed out on the desk. "And you handed over the kid? How dare you."

"Oh, God," Janice says. "I'm so sorry." She breaks down completely, tears streaming down her cheeks.

"Enough," Hernandez says, irritated.

She levels the handgun at Janice…

BAM.

CHAPTER 28

Janice's head snaps back, then forward. Her body slumps over dead. Startled, Jamal wails as the gunshot rings out. Patrisse and I watch helplessly as Hernandez pulls the kid into her arms.

"Now, now," Hernandez says, petting his head with her free hand, the gun still smoking in her other. "It's okay. Everything's okay." She rocks him back and forth, then smiles at Patrisse and me. "Aren't children precious?" she asks. "You know, Evans, he's about the same age you were when you entered the hammer program. What do you think? Does he have what it takes?"

Her gaze lingers on me, but I say nothing.

Hernandez chuckles, then squeezes the kid. "You know, you have your father's eyes," she tells him. "Has anybody ever told you that?"

Jamal shrugs, but his attention is fixed on Janice's lifeless body — on the bright red blood dripping to the floor. Hernandez grows impatient.

"It's too bad you'll never see him again," she says, spiteful.

Jamal blinks. He looks at her critically. "Is he dead?"

Hernandez shrugs. "I'm afraid so, pal."

Jamal glances at me, then Patrisse, confused.

"You monster," Patrisse says, glaring at Hernandez.

"It's the truth, isn't it?" Hernandez asks. "Or don't you think he can handle it?" She raises an eyebrow toward me. "And what about Evans here," she says. "Can he handle it?"

Jamal looks between the women, then me. Leaning forward, I pull the action figures from my pocket and set them on the desk, positioning them with the others.

"Why don't you go play with them on the sofa," I say.

Jamal nods, then pries himself from Hernandez's grasp. As he gathers his toys, Hernandez picks up the action figure that he'd given to me.

"Mind if I keep this one?" she asks.

Jamal hesitates. He looks at me, and I nod — I just want the kid out of her reach. With my permission, he hurries by Janice's body, careful not to glance at the gore, and heads to the furniture arrangement, dumping his toys on the coffee table.

Hernandez, she studies the action figure in her hand, then shifts her gaze toward me. "So, Evans," she says. "Can you handle the truth?" I don't respond. I don't even blink. Whatever her game is, it has begun. Hernandez smiles, smug and confident. "The truth is," she says. "I couldn't be more pleased with you."

Me, I think of the scramjet. Any minute now, it should be airborne, punching into lower Earth orbit. And within moments after that, it should be arching back down toward the tower. We'll see how pleased she's with me then. But for now, I need to figure a way out of here.

"Oh, really?" I ask, stalling for time. "How's that?" — keeping her talking is my best strategy for now. I'm only half-listening as Hernandez continues.

She holds up the action figure, her palm as a pedestal.

"Society was built on hero worship," she says. "As much today as when we were hunter-gatherers. It's human nature. To rule or be ruled. To subjugate or be subjugated." She closes her fingers around the toy and leans toward me. "Do you remember the last time you were in this office? The last time we spoke? It was before you went on this little journey-of-discovery." With this, she has my attention again. "I told you to make a statement, didn't I? I asked you to make it big." She chuckles. "And you didn't disappoint."

I blink. I glance at Patrisse, uncertain. Remembering that conversation, right here in this office: yeah, that's exactly what she said to me.

Hernandez laughs. "Don't look so surprised, dear," she says.

Me, no longer in the mood to play games, I break my silence. "What are you talking about?"

"This storyline," Hernandez says, playing with the action figure on her desk, making it walk along the tabletop. "It was all my idea, really. But we've been developing it for years now." Her eyes flick toward me. "Your rebellion, the resistance, this climax — this is your raison d'être, my dear... your reason to exist."

Me, I'm thinking of Gorman, moments before his death: was he trying to warn me?

Hernandez looks out the window at the city below. She nods, pleased. "The ratings have been fantastic. Everybody's watching, their eyes glued to their screens. And not just primetime. I'm talking from the moment they wake to the moment they fall asleep; they are following your every move. Even out West," she adds, impressed. "In California, they lifted their ban on our programming. And they're just as engrossed. They love it. It has everything: redemption, revenge, revolution. Hell, the network hasn't had ratings like this since... well, since D.C. went up in flames." She looks at me, glowing. "This is a generational event," she says, then leans toward me. "Taylor Evans, you may single-handedly bring this country back together again."

Me, I'm refusing to accept this. Hernandez can't be saying what I think she's saying. I look at Patrisse, desperate.

"It's bullshit," Patrisse says. "All of it."

Hernandez glances between us, then laughs. "It's Jonah and the Whale, Evans. The Hero's Journey. And here you are, back where it all began, born anew." She looks me over. Realizing I'm still lost, she shakes her head with pity. "What I'm saying is... it's all part of the show."

That I hear. Stunned, I sit, unable to blink or breathe. A quick montage flashes in my mind. Every moment I've endured over the last few days, each one more cinematic and exciting than the last...

Patrisse, she jumps out of her chair and grabs my arm. She shakes me back to the present. To the here and now. Not Hernandez's delusional fantasy world.

"This is it, Evans," Patrisse says. "She's tricking you. Everything she's saying, it's bullshit meant to confuse you. They're breaking you down to control you."

Hernandez scoffs. "Did you really think the resistance was real, Evans?" she asks. "Do you think I'd let something

like that exist? A threat to the network? To this," she
says, waving her hands toward the building around us.
"Everything I've built. Everything I've accomplished. Would
I risk that, even for a second?"

She laughs at the seeming absurdity.

Me, I think of the people I've met. The world I discovered. Jackson and Janice. Jamal and Dean…

"Actors," Hernandez says, reading my mind. "All
of them."

"What about…" I say, but Hernandez is way
ahead of me.

"Months of planning and preparation. Rewrites and
rehearsals," Hernandez sighs as if these details bore her. "But
the blood's real." She points at Janice. "There's no substitute
for that. Nothing sells a scene like real blood and guts. But
as for your new *friends*," she says, air-quoting the word
friends. She shrugs. "Central casting, buddy."

"That's ridiculous," Patrisse says, glaring at her. Patrisse
turns to me. "Don't believe a word…"

"Ridiculous?" Hernandez asks, cutting her off. "Does
this look ridiculous to you?" She smiles confidently and,
with a quick hand gesture, activates the video screen. The
monitor descends from the ceiling and flickers on.

On-screen, a social media profile pops up for Patrisse… only it's not Patrisse; the name is different. Hernandez sits up straight and clears her throat.

"Patrisse Flynn," she says. "Real name: Bree Gavin." A series of photos scroll by, pictures from throughout Patrisse's life. School photos, holiday photos, a graduation portrait. Hernandez sneers as the network's own file appears on the screen. "And look at this," she says. "We cast her almost six months ago today." She turns to me. "Tell me, Evans. When do you remember first seeing Miss Flynn?"

"Fake," Patrisse shouts. "All of it. They salvaged my hard drives and pulled old photos. It doesn't mean shit."

Hernandez nods, then shrugs. "But wait, there's more." With a swipe of her hand, video footage slides onto the screen. "What's this?" Hernandez asks with mock surprise.

In the grainy footage, Jackson appears seated at a table, script in hand. "Looks like you could use a friend," he says, reading. I recognize the dialogue immediately: it's the first thing Jackson said to me on the dock the morning after I fled the hammer.

Off-camera, somebody reads along with him. "Who are you?" the person asks — that was my line.

"A friend," Jackson reads, devoid of all emotion or character — this is a rehearsal of some sort. A script reading. Me, my jaw drops. I glance between Hernandez and Patrisse, but the footage cuts to another setup...

This time, it's Dean at a table, script in hand. "I bet you'll call us godless next," he reads. "Atheists, perhaps? Or whatever the network finds more triggering with its audience these days." Dean crosses his arms in mock-annoyance — this was my first interaction with the man back at the compound.

I turn to Patrisse. "What the hell is going on here?" I ask.

"Deep fakes," Patrisse says. "Nothing new. I told you we shouldn't have come here. This was a mistake."

But for me, my head is spinning. I look at Hernandez. She beams back at me. "What about my mother?" I ask.

Hernandez smirks, then shakes her head. "Another actor, Evans," she says. "Just some much-needed character motivation to kick off the third act."

I glance at Patrisse puzzled — has she lost her confidence? Is she breaking character? But if she is an actor, why isn't she backing down? Why not just come clean, especially now? I lean forward and drop my head into my hands, confused and frustrated. I feel my perception of reality slipping through my fingers. Patrisse, she warned me about this. She told me to cling to the truth.

But what is true?

Hernandez keeps swiping through more and more behind-the-scenes footage. I catch myself crying in my shower — the same footage Dean had shown me back at the compound. There I am on the Ben Franklin Bridge walking into the city to rescue Patrisse. There's Jamal and me back in the garage. The kid hands me the action figure…

"You're one of the good guys," Jamal says on-screen.

Jamal, here in the office with us, stares at himself, transfixed.

Hernandez pauses the video. "This," she says, engrossed in the footage. "This sentimental shit. Audiences really connect with this. Silly, sure. But it shows you got heart, Evans. I'm telling you: you nailed it here."

As Hernandez swipes through more footage, Patrisse eyes me sitting next to her, shaking her head. "This is how they do it," she says, repeating what she told me in the elevator. "This is how they get you back."

Hernandez stops swiping, then snorts. On-screen, Patrisse and I are back in the elevator — this footage, it's from just a few minutes ago. We draw toward each other, then kiss. Hernandez pauses the footage.

"A little forced, wasn't it?" she asks. Patrisse and I stare at her blankly. "Here, your buddy Jackson lay dead at your feet," she says, pointing at the screen. She glances at Patrisse. "And you, Patrisse, weren't you his lover?"

Patrisse blinks and then looks at me, uncomfortable.

Hernandez laughs. "It's been pretty vague, I'll give you that," Hernandez says. "But then… that kiss." Hernandez looks at me. "Didn't that seem forced to you?"

I don't say anything. Hernandez shakes her head, amused. "It didn't matter what you said here; she was going to kiss you regardless," she says. "Why?" She glances between us, waiting for an answer. "Because the audience eats it up, that's why."

"This is absurd," Patrisse says, slamming her palm against the desk. Hernandez snickers at the theatrics, but Patrisse continues. "This footage, it's laughable. Everything she's saying, Evans, is a lie. But it's all she's got. This is her last-minute Hail Mary to rein you back in."

"Is that right?" Hernandez asks, but Patrisse ignores her.

"I'm not an actor," she says. "You know that. We fought side by side. The resistance… it's real. You were with us. Janice… she's dead, Evans. She's not an actor. Look at Jamal," Patrisse points at the kid, and he stares back at us, perplexed. "He's not an actor, Evans. He's a child. That's Jackson's little boy. *The Eagle's Hammer* killed his mother." She looks at me, pleading. "This is real, Evans. Me and you. And Jamal. This is real. You know that, right?"

I stare at her wide-eyed, then nod.

Patrisse points at Hernandez. "I told you they would trick you. I told you they'd twist the truth until it breaks apart and crumbles. Don't listen to her, Evans. Don't listen to a word she says. It's bullshit. All of it. This is a desperate attempt to rein you back in, to regain control of you. Because they need you. The network needs you to control the people out there." Patrisse points out the window at the city. "The only way to end this nightmare is to stop listening to them." Patrisse glares at Hernandez. "Stop listening to her."

"Patrisse," Hernandez says, standing up. "You're fired."

She raises her gun at Patrisse, then pulls the trigger...

BAM.

CHAPTER 29

Patrisse collapses into her chair. Me, I jump out of mine and cradle her in my arms. But she's dead. Jamal screams from the sofa — the horror this child has now witnessed is staggering. All at the hands of Hanna Hernandez, evil incarnate.

Hernandez watches my anguish, loving it. "That girl needs to learn when to break character," she says, sitting back down. "But what can I say? We have very convincing non-disclosure agreements."

Patrisse goes cold in my arms, and I glare at Hernandez. Images of strangling her flash in my mind. Perhaps I can throw her through these windows and let her fall to her death. Then I think of the scramjet...

"Don't worry," Hernandez says, smirking. "We'll recast her." Jamal, his cries continue unabated. "Shut up," Hernandez shouts at him. "Shut up, now."

She's going to kill him too, I realize. Hernandez catches me glancing at the gun in her hand. She shakes her head — not at the thought I may take the weapon, but seemingly at the fact that I still think she's full of shit... *which I do.*

Patrisse was right. The photos, the footage: that can easily be manipulated and faked. And there are cameras everywhere, so pulling footage of me walking across the bridge or talking to Jamal isn't impossible. Probably from the minute I ran, Hernandez and the network had this conspiracy in the works, lest they admit that somebody, even me, had gotten the better of them.

"Still not swallowing this, are you?" Hernandez asks. "I apologize for keeping you out of the loop, but believe me, that made it all the more authentic." She chuckles. "Weren't you curious why it was so easy to escape the way you did? Or why you were able to thwart the hammer at every encounter?"

I blink. Being Taylor Evans, it's hard to imagine anybody being better than me. But the idea that I had a handicapped advantage doesn't sit right. No, the other hammers — Riggs and CJ included — they had it out for me. And Milner, he wanted blood.

"It was all part of the show," Hernandez answers. She gestures toward me. "You, Taylor Evans. You are the show. You are *The Eagle's Hammer.*"

I look at Patrisse in my arms and think of everything she told me — that Hernandez and the network would do absolutely anything to rope me back in. I set her down gently in the chair, then squat next to her, looking at her for what may be the last time. She's the leader this country needs. But like so many of those who were fit to lead, she wound up dead.

Hernandez grows impatient. She clears her throat and stands. "Every generation grows weary of the societal constraints placed upon them," she says, sounding every bit the CEO — this is a pitch. "Every generation seeks to push forward. But controlling that desire, manipulating the people to contain that progress: we've perfected that strategy. I present to you the Trucast Corporation," she says proudly. "No finer mechanism of control has ever existed. From internet access to content distribution, we succeed where all other empires before us — the Romans, the Turks, the Zhou — all faltered."

Hernandez approaches the window. She looks out at the city below. "We might as well be their air, their lungs. Without us, they are nothing."

Me, I stand up and cross my arms. Hernandez admires my reflection in the glass, handsome and stoic: just the way she likes me. Smirking, she picks up the expensive bottle of champagne she's had chilling on ice and turns toward me.

"Here's the thing," she says. "The people want a revolution. Every generation does. And they want you — Taylor Evans — to lead it." She pops the bottle, delighting at the fizz. "The people, they need it. All of this: you, the resistance, the do-gooding. It makes them feel like they're doing something with their pathetic little lives, even though they're just sitting on their asses watching you. They will forever consume the reality we choose to feed them... as long as they're entertained."

Hernandez picks up two crystal flutes and the bottle in one hand, then saunters around the desk with the gun in her other. She hesitates, looking over the dead bodies of Janice and Patrisse with disdain. Then, using the butt of the pistol, she pushes Patrisse's arm off the armrest and sits.

"Now, don't get me wrong," she says. "If I could throw them all in one big gas chamber, I would. But what kind of ratings could we expect then? Right?" She laughs, then sets the two flutes on the desk. She pours the champagne, careful not to spill it over. "No, this is for the best. The network, the hammer: it's tough love, sure. But it's effective, isn't it?" She waves a limp hand toward the window, toward the city outside. "As long as they're engaged, they come back. And back. And back. Wanting more of whatever we're feeding them. Whether it's fear or hope, it's all the same."

She hands me a flute. I reflexively take it into my hand, feeling the cool crystal against my skin. And that's when I realize we're not alone up here on the Eight-Four…

Glancing at my reflection in the massive windows, I see *them* stepping out of the shadows behind me, converging toward me. Their glazed-over gazes are more expectant than ever; my victims have joined us. And at this point, I'm happy to see them.

Hernandez holds up her glass. "To Taylor Evans, the nation's savior," she says, clinking mine.

But my thoughts are elsewhere, as they always are when the murdered horde comes to haunt me. Hernandez, she has no idea. She's in her own little world, happy to pat herself on the back for a job well done.

"I see this running two or three seasons, tops," she says, sipping the champagne. "You don't want to drag a revolution out too long. People lose interest."

My eyes shift to her. I consider what she's saying, what she's propositioning. Something tells me President Norton is at the crux of it.

"How?" I ask, curious to know what her endgame is. An open-ended question, sure. But I want to keep her talking.

Hernandez scoffs. "It's simple," she says. "We tell the people what is truth. That's big T truth. Not what's true. There's a difference. And the people, they accept it. Take, for example… Norton." Upon saying the president's name, she scowls. "He's president because we say he is. If we say nothing, he is nothing. If we tell them that you are a traitor…" She pokes me with a finger. "If we tell them you're a monster, then the villagers come to burn you at the stake. They'll drag your corpse through the streets like any fallen tyrant. But…"

Hernandez giggles. "If we tell them you're a patriot. If we tell them you're their repentant savior, sent from God to lift America to a higher realm of existence… they'll worship you until the day you die. Beautiful, isn't it? They express their new, enlightened aesthetic without discarding their materialistic addictions. They still go to work. They still incur debt. And we still milk them dry with interest." She smiles, content. "Rinse and repeat," she adds.

"What about Norton?" I ask, genuinely intrigued. I think of the National Guard that Norton has at his disposal. I think of the Secret Service sworn to protect him, the President of the United States.

"Norton," she says, nodding. "He's out there right now in that stupid fortress train of his. He's already on the run, Evans. It's perfect. It's made for TV. And you, Taylor Evans — *The Taylor Evans* — you get to hunt him down to the delight of millions of faithful viewers. And when you find him…" Hernandez looks at me, eyebrows raised. "It's hammer time."

I stare back at her, expressionless. Jamal's sobs have thinned out. And the smell of gun smoke has dissipated. Outside, rain patters the windows.

In here, Hanna sets her flute down and leans toward me, placing a hand on my leg. With the handgun, she points at the US flag behind her desk. The barrel waves indiscriminately at the stars and stripes as she talks.

"A revolution," she says. "Of our making. A reboot. For this entire country. And at the center of it all: you. *The Eagle's Hammer* himself."

I close my eyes, imagining the life she's offering. The cameras following me, the people adoring me. Candis, my wife, welcoming me back with open arms — a nightmare, all of it. Truly a nightmare. But this whole thing is preposterous, and maybe that's the point. Flip it all upside down. As she said, it's a reboot.

"No," I say, shaking my head. "This is bullshit. You didn't know I'd run. You didn't know I'd return. Don't act like you pulled this off."

Hernandez eyes me like I'm a dog performing tricks. "How cute," she says. "But naive. You ran because we wanted you to. You're here now because we wanted you here. Everything you do, you do because we made you do it. Everything you are, you are because we shaped you. You, me, all of us — we are products of our environment. Behavior is shaped by environment." She looks me over, pitying me. "There is nothing original about you. There's no decision you make that wasn't predetermined. If unchecked, unregulated neoliberalism has taught us anything in the last century, it's that freewill just does not exist, my dear."

Hernandez reaches for my clenched fist, bringing it up between us. Then she does something that takes me completely by surprise: she offers me the gun. I blink, staring at the weapon — is this a trick?

"Take it," she says. "It's heavy, and you look better holding it anyway."

My fingers slide around the cold-steel handle. The weapon feels good in my hand...

"No," I say. "I chose to be here." I immediately place the barrel to her temple — she simply smiles back at me. "I chose to put this gun to your head," I say, desperately willing myself to pull the trigger. The steel is pressed against her skin. All I have to do is squeeze, and I finish this madness once and for all...

"Think hard, Evans," she says. "The family that night, your target the night you ran. Do you remember them?"

I picture the woman standing in her living room, the children cowering behind her, crying... *Kill target and all associates.*

I nod. "Yeah. And I chose not to kill them."

Hernandez giggles. "Did you? Or had we been molding you for that moment for years? Since the day you were born, we've been shaping you. Your thoughts, your desires, your fears. All of you is our making. We knew you were cracking. We knew about all the times you'd cry in the shower. The brewing doubts and anxieties in your heart. We knew you wanted to escape because we planted those seeds in your head. And we knew the strings to pull to get you back. Patrisse. Jamal. The resistance."

She lets that point sink in.

"Now pull the trigger, just like I want you to," she says.

But me, I try to. Staring into her eyes, I so badly want to blow her brains out. I even position the gun just as Milner instructed. Up and out. The gore will be glorious...

But I can't do it. My hand, the gun, it goes limp.

Hernandez loves it. She reaches up and takes the pistol from me. *She owns me. Completely.* Out of sadistic curiosity, simply to see how I'll react, she levels the gun at Jamal.

Me, I'm frozen in terror — *Oh no, not the kid!*

Hernandez pulls the trigger… but the chamber clicks empty. And she cackles in my face.

I'm stunned. But not at how monstrous Hernandez is or that human life means nothing to her. I'm stunned because there wasn't another bullet in the chamber. So even if I had pulled the trigger, she wouldn't have died…

Hernandez is playing it off as a laugh, but to me, that's significant. My mind races through what this means. Here is Hernandez telling me she has complete control over me… only she doesn't? She clearly didn't trust me not to pull the trigger — to not blow her brains out.

Does that mean all of her control… it's all bullshit, just like Patrisse said?

Yes, they say, their reflection in the window— my victims. The horde, they're here for the main event. All of them. My gaze shifts from one face to another. They're all here, and then some. Joaquin Rogers, he's here, smiling at me. He's proud of me. Jackson and Zack: they're here too, my friends. Real friends. There are thousands of them, and they all want the same thing. But I search their faces until I find her: Jamal's mother. When I spot her, the others clear out of the way, and she steps forward.

Do it, she says, commanding me. *Finish this.*

Hernandez, she can't see them, not as I can. And here, for so long, I was afraid of them, terrified of them. I thought they wanted to drag me off to hell. But it wasn't me they wanted. It was Milner. And Hernandez. And the network.

So now, I do what I should have done long ago. Just like I would give into Hernandez and the network night after night, murder after murder, I give in to the horde.

No longer thinking, I simply do.

You put a weapon in my hand...

Hernandez, she flashes that million-dollar smile of hers. She has no idea what's going on in my head.

"This is America, Evans," she says. "Your America."

And with that, she clinks her flute against mine, celebrating the world she doesn't realize is crashing around her. Me, I take the flute and smash it against the desk, splattering the champagne as I shatter the crystal at its stem. Then, with that dangerously sharp edge, I stab Hernandez in the neck, piercing her carotid.

It happens fast, lightning fast. But for a moment, for a brief sliver of time, I see it. I see the same look on her face as I did the hundreds of people she forced me to kill. I see her fear. It's the one thing I know with absolute certainty. Fear is my specialty. And they — the ghosts of all the network's victims — they feed off it.

Just like Hermann Göring, Hernandez isn't a monster. She's flesh and blood, like you and me. And even the most powerful person in the world is just that: a person. They're as weak and vulnerable as everybody else. They die just as easily. Hanna Hernandez probably never would have accepted that fact. But now, she doesn't have a choice.

I watch her as she pulls the stem from her neck, shocked that I would have the audacity to harm her. But even that stern expression gives way. Her face softens, and she stumbles into the window. With every beat of her heart, blood squirts onto the glass — Milner would love this.

Jamal, he watches silently as Hernandez cups the wound with her hands. But it's pointless. Blood seeps around her fingers, running down her sleeve. Her face flushed, she drops to her knees. Her eyes dart about — from me to the kid, to me again, knowing neither of us is about to help her. Then, with finality, she keels over, falling into the puddle beneath her.

Me, I watch as blood soaks into her white suit.

CHAPTER 30

You, you were there with your kid clutched in your arms when the network went dark. Like me, desperate and confused, you started flipping through the channels to figure out what the hell was going on. The two of us, both you and I, we saw the same damn thing...

"... a one-man revolution..."

"... an American hero..."

"... administration refuses to comment..."

"... who will play him in the movie?"

If you think you're confused, try standing where I am: in a pool of Hanna Hernandez's blood on the eighty-fourth floor of Trucast Tower. Jamal, he's by my side, equally perplexed, as I surf through the channels.

They're gone, in case you were wondering. My victims — the horde of the undead that has haunted me since my days of killing began — they're gone. I guess they got what they wanted after all. Unless, of course, like the woman in my dreams, they too were just programmed memories and hallucinations. Just another string to control me with.

Was that woman my mother? I don't know.

Was Patrisse an actress? I don't know.

Is the resistance real? I have no idea.

Was this all orchestrated from the get-go? You tell me.

The one thing I do know: I'm a pawn. I've always been a pawn. Like the action figures clutched in Jamal's hands, somebody has always had me in their grip. Was it Hernandez? Maybe. It sure seemed like it to me, but again: what the hell do I know?

Could somebody else have been calling the shots? Could Hernandez have also been a pawn? Now, my head really starts to hurt. Me, I glance about her office, spotting all the locations cameras could be hidden. Where does the show end and real-life begin?

I guess this is what I have to find out.

Me, I've concluded that the scramjet isn't coming. Whether Patrisse failed to program the autonomous jet, or the network managed to abort its suicide mission — or she was simply an actor, and none of this was real to begin

307

with — the fiery destruction of Trucast Tower and all it represents seems unlikely. Bummer.

I swoop Jamal into my arms, and we head toward the elevators — I think we'll skip the one with Jackson's dead body still inside it. For what it's worth, the kid never broke character. Feeling his skin against mine, I know he's real. And his innocence, his sincerity, it gives me hope that his father, and Patrisse, and the resistance were also real; that everything Hernandez said was bullshit.

But if I've learned anything, it's not to get your hopes up.

I press the button for the lobby, and as the elevator descends, I consider all the various possibilities awaiting me at the bottom. A battalion of nats may be down there, armed to the teeth. At President Norton's orders, I may swiftly be slaughtered. The thought appeals to me. On the other hand, if I'm to believe the network's news coverage, a crowd of supporters may have already gathered, as they do after every episode of *The Eagle's Hammer*.

I can picture them, their mouths agape in ecstasy, screaming and snapping selfies...

Nobody lives in the moment anymore — not unless you put a gun to their head.

Lastly, perhaps nobody is down there, and the lobby is empty. Maybe everything, all the drama and intrigue, including my public adulation, has all been network spin...

Like Hernandez said: it's all part of the show.

As the elevator approaches the ground floor, I close my eyes. I begin to hear *The Eagle's Hammer* theme music. It's the underscore that typically proceeds the end credits. This story is almost finished, for now. But before it ends, I think of you. If you are out there, it's probably time to get your kid to bed. It's time to kiss your husband goodnight. And, perhaps for the first time in your life, you're hopeful for tomorrow.

Then again, you may not even exist. Like my mother or my horde of victims, you could all just be figments of my overactive imagination.

As for me, I'm not even sure I care anymore.

The elevator chimes. And the doors slide open.

THE END

If you enjoyed this novel, please leave
a review so that others will be encouraged to read it
— the author thanks you.

ABOUT THE AUTHOR

Christopher Kügler lives in central Pennsylvania with his wife and two dogs. He's worked in broadcast television for way too long and now enjoys writing novels.

Chris loves hearing from his readers.
You can find him at
www.christopherkugler.com
and on TikTok *@cklockwork*

ALSO BY CHRISTOPHER KÜGLER

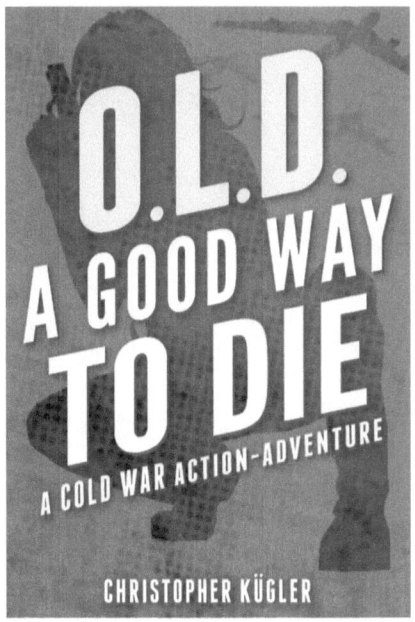

What readers are saying:

"An impressive, ambitious debut sure to appeal to fans of high-action spy novels."
J.L. Delozier, author of *The Photo Thief*

"Part history lesson, part action-adventure, and part warning for the future -- this book is exactly the read we all need right now."
Goodreads reader

"To anyone who grew up in the 80s, this is your history as you never saw it before."
Amazon customer

"A gripping, page-turning, spy novel!"
Amazon customer